LOUISE'S CHANCE

A Selection of Titles from Sarah R. Shaber

The Professor Simon Shaw Series

SIMON SAID
SNIPE HUNT
THE FUGITIVE KING
THE BUG FUNERAL
SHELL GAME

The Louise Pearlie Series

LOUISE'S WAR *
LOUISE'S GAMBLE *
LOUISE'S DILEMMA *
LOUISE'S BLUNDER *
LOUISE'S CHANCE *

* *available from Severn House*

LOUISE'S CHANCE

Sarah R. Shaber

This first world edition published 2015
in Great Britain and the USA by
SEVERN HOUSE PUBLISHERS LTD of
19 Cedar Road, Sutton, Surrey, England, SM2 5DA.
Trade paperback edition first published
in Great Britain and the USA 2015 by
SEVERN HOUSE PUBLISHERS LTD.

British Library Cataloguing in Publication Data

Shaber, Sarah R. author.
  Louise's chance
  1. Pearlie, Louise (Fictitious character)–Fiction.
  2. United States. Office of Strategic Services–
  Employees-Fiction. 3. World War, 1939-1945-Prisoners
  and prisons–Fiction. 4. Suspense fiction.
  I. Title
  813.6-dc23

ISBN-13: 978-07278-8552-4 (cased)
ISBN-13: 978-1-84751-661-9 (trade paper)
ISBN-13: 978-1-78010-715-8 (e-book)

All Severn House titles are printed on acid-free paper.

Severn House Publishers support The Forest Stewardship Council™ [FSC™],
the leading international forest certification organisation. All our titles that
are printed on FSC certified paper carry the FSC logo.

MIX
Paper from
responsible sources
FSC® C013056

Typeset by Palimpsest Book Production Ltd.,
Falkirk, Stirlingshire, Scotland.
Printed and bound in Great Britain by
TJ International, Padstow, Cornwall

In memory of Ken Tutterow, President and CEO of the Children's Home Society of North Carolina from 1990 to 2014, beloved friend, leader and advocate for the children of North Carolina. It was his mission to promote the right of every child to a permanent, safe and loving family. Thousands of foster children, adopted children and adoptive parents are leading happy lives today because of his good work.

ACKNOWLEDGEMENTS

With each new book I find myself thanking the same people for their support and encouragement. My husband, Steve, daughter, Katie and son, Sam, are my closest friends and the best cheering squad anyone could have. I can't imagine my life without the friendship and advice of my writing buddies: Margaret Maron, Bren Witchger, Diane Chamberlain, Kathy Trocheck (Mary Kay Andrews), Katy Munger and Alexandra Sokoloff. My friend Vicky Bijur is the best agent in the world. And I am forever grateful that Quail Ridge Books and Music is my home bookstore.

ONE

I sensed the assault coming before it happened, throwing my arms out in front of me to deflect the impact. A big person, bigger than me, landed next to me on the bed. Yards of rayon washed over and covered me. 'Louise!' the heap said. 'Help me!'

It was Ada, home from her job as a clarinetist in the Statler Hotel house band. And I was in my own bed, startled from a deep sleep. Ada was late. She must have stayed to party with the band after their gig was over. Or with one of her many admirers, as she so often did.

'Darn it, Ada,' I said, reaching over to my bedside table and clicking on my lamp. I glanced at my clock. 'It's two in the morning!'

She clung to me, her arms tight around me. Mascara trailed down her cheeks to her chin, and her bright red lipstick was smeared around her mouth. Her peroxide blond hair had fallen out of her snood and tangled at her shoulder. I put my arms around her. I could feel her trembling.

'I'm so frightened!' Ada said.

'What on earth is the matter?' I said. I pulled my bedcovers aside so Ada could slip into the warm bed with me. I could smell gin on her breath.

'They're bringing them here!' she said. 'What if he's with them?'

I gripped her arms, shaking her slightly.

'Calm down,' I said. 'Who is bringing who here? Who is *he*?'

Her breathing slowed a bit.

'German prisoners of war,' she said. 'Thousands of them are coming to the States! The government is going to build camps for them all over the country!'

'I know,' I said. Most of Rommel's army in North Africa

had been captured four months ago. Hundreds of thousands of German prisoners of war waited in temporary camps and collection centers to be shipped to permanent Allied POW camps. Some of the temporary camps were no more than corrals, where hungry, thirsty and exhausted Axis prisoners lived surrounded by barbed wire under the desert sun. The Allies simply were not prepared to house them. They couldn't all be shipped to Britain; the British could barely feed themselves.

'What if Rein is one of them? A man I was with tonight said that fifty-eight German soldiers have already arrived at Fort Meade! Some of them are Luftwaffe!'

Now I understood. Before the war Ada was married to Rein Hermann, a German airline pilot based in New York City. He flew the New York–Berlin route for Lufthansa. At first Ada and Rein's marriage was a happy one, but then Rein became more and more intrigued by Adolf Hitler and the Nazi Party. His interest grew into an obsession until the couple fought about politics constantly.

Then one day when Ava met Rein's usual Lufthansa flight at LaGuardia Field an unfamiliar pilot disembarked from the airplane. Rein had remained behind in Germany. He wrote Ada that he'd joined the Luftwaffe. He pleaded with her to move to Germany, but of course she refused. Since then she'd lived in terror that someone would discover she was the wife of a Nazi officer. She dropped the second 'n' from her last name and moved from New York City to Washington DC. Ada couldn't even divorce Rein for fear of attracting attention to herself. I understood her fear. It was likely she'd be interned in a camp for German-Americans, if her marriage was discovered. Ada had told me her story during a weak moment and I swore to keep her secret. And I would, even if hell froze over.

'What am I going to do?' Ada asked. 'What if Rein is here and tells the FBI about me?'

'Dearie,' I said, throwing back the covers and struggling past Ada to get out of the bed, 'it's not very likely that Rein would be one of just fifty-eight prisoners, is it? Out of, what, thousands of Luftwaffe pilots? If he is a POW he could be imprisoned at some other camp. Or in Europe. You don't know if he was captured at all; you don't even know, if he was stationed in North Africa.'

'Rein would inform on me if he had the chance,' Ada said, sitting up on my bed and dangling her long legs over the edge. 'He would relish ruining my life in return for not joining him in Germany. God, I wish he was dead!'

A sentiment I had heard her express many times. I didn't blame her. I pulled on my dressing gown.

'Where are you going?' Ada asked. 'Don't leave me!'

'Getting a tablet for you from Phoebe,' I said. Phoebe Holcombe was our landlady.

I tiptoed down the second-floor hall of our boarding house to Phoebe's room and tapped on her bedroom door.

'Phoebe,' I called out. 'I'm sorry to bother you. Can I come in?'

Her sleepy voice answered me. 'What is it, Louise?' she asked. 'Is everything all right?'

'Yes,' I said, slipping into her room. 'But Ada came home from work terribly upset. Can I give her one of your tablets?'

'Of course,' Phoebe said, raising her head from her silk-covered pillow. Her grey hair was done up in old-fashioned pin curls. A nightlight glowed next to her bed. 'Tell her I hope she feels better.' She lowered her head back on to her pillow and appeared to fall right back to sleep. She must have taken a sleep aid herself.

I found the Nembutal in her medicine cabinet next to a glass bottle of laudanum. I shook a tablet into my hand, briefly considered taking one myself and decided against it for fear I'd be sleepy all day tomorrow.

Back in my room I found Ada right where I'd left her, curled up in my bed like a child.

'Here,' I said, pulling her to a seating position. I handed her the tablet and the tumbler of water I kept on my bedside table. 'Take this; you'll feel better and be able to sleep.'

Ada swallowed the pill and handed the empty tumbler back to me.

'What do you think?' she asked. 'About Rein?'

I sat on the edge of the bed and took her hand.

'I think it's unlikely that Rein would be in that group of German prisoners sent to Fort Meade, even if he's been captured. Dozens of POW camps are being built all over the country. Besides, if Rein had been captured wouldn't he disclose that he was married to an American woman right away? I mean, if he was going to use it to his advantage? You haven't heard anything, have you?'

'No,' Ada said. 'I haven't. Not a thing.'

She gripped me hand hard, her eyes pleading. 'Can you find out? If Rein is a prisoner of war here in the States?'

'What?' I said, taken aback. 'How can I do that? I'm just a file clerk.'

'I'm not deaf and blind. You know things most of us don't,' Ada said. 'You must work for some important government agency. I bet you can find out if Rein is in the country.'

Maybe I could, I thought. I worked for the Office of Strategic Services, the United States' spy agency. If there was a list of the names of German POWs floating around the office I might be able to locate it. I wasn't going to promise Ada that, though.

'I'll try,' I said. 'But I don't have a high security clearance. Mostly I move paper around and shove it into file cabinets to turn yellow with age, that's all.' I patted her hand. 'Look, go wash your face and go to bed. I've got to get some more sack time. Some people work mornings, you know.'

'They should just put all of them on a rusty ship, send it out into the middle of the ocean and torpedo it,' Henry said, tossing the morning *Washington Times-Herald* on to the sideboard as he came into the breakfast room.

'Who?' I asked. If someone didn't ask Henry what he meant by one of his rhetorical statements we would just have to listen to him try again to get our attention.

'Those prisoners of war they're bringing over here,' Henry said. 'Germans and Italians. Hey, do you know what the Italian salute is?' When he got no response, he raised both hands in the air and grinned.

Milt, Phoebe's oldest son, who was adding raisins and milk to his oatmeal with one hand, his empty left sleeve hanging from his side, grimaced and took Henry's bait. 'We have to abide by the Geneva Convention,' he said. 'If we don't the Germans have an excuse to treat Allied prisoners badly.'

'Milt Senior and I went to Italy on our honeymoon,' Phoebe said, trying to steer the conversation away from the war. 'Lovely country, lovely people.'

I'd gotten where I was today by keeping my mouth shut. I did my best not to join in conversations about the war with anyone, much less Henry. I had Top Secret clearance, and I didn't even want to give myself an opportunity to say something I shouldn't. But ridiculing the Italians was unfair. Yes, their soldiers threw down their weapons and deserted in droves. Yes, the Italian government surrendered to the Allies the day before the Allies landed in Salerno. But that was because most Italians despised Mussolini and Hitler and refused to die for them, not because they were cowards.

Milt reached across the table for the spoon in the bowl of oatmeal. 'Can I finish this?' he asked.

'Ada hasn't eaten yet,' Phoebe said.

'I doubt she'll be downstairs to breakfast,' I said. 'She came in very late last night.'

Milt scraped out the rest of the oatmeal into his bowl. It had been several months since he came home from the Pacific without his left arm and moved into the attic bedroom with Henry. He hadn't fully recovered from his ordeal, but had found a job and had begun to go out with old friends. He wasn't drinking as much lately, either.

I stood up from the table. 'I'm off, then,' I said. 'Everyone have a good day. I'll see you tonight. Henry, if you're finished with your paper, could I have it?'

'Sure,' he said.

I slipped Henry's newspaper off the sideboard and took it with me to the bus stop.

The heat of summer lingered. I walked to the bus stop wearing my dark glasses, a khaki dress styled much like a military uniform (as was the fashion among civilian war workers) and a straw fedora. But every now and then I noticed a gold or scarlet leaf peeking out between green tree branches. A welcome breeze wafted inland from the Potomac. Autumn was coming. It would bring relief from the awful heat and monster mosquitos of summer, thank God, but then winter would inevitably follow. If heating oil was rationed again, as I was sure it would be, the second floor of 'Two Trees', our boarding house, would be cold as a witch's tit, as my grandfather used to say.

I found an empty seat on the bus next to a middle-aged man who wore a sash with the triangular emblem of the Civil Defense and held a helmet in his lap. He was sound asleep, his head resting on the seat back, snoring lightly. I opened my newspaper with minimal rustling so as not to disturb him.

The front page was full of news about the Italian government's surrender. But it also quoted General Eisenhower, who said that the Allies faced a 'bitter battle' against the Germans in Italy. Field Marshal General Albert Kesselring, as 'commander in chief in the South', declared martial law in all of German-occupied Italy. German-controlled radio broadcast a grim warning that all Italians who did not comply with Nazi rule would be executed. Even the Vatican prepared for the worst. The Pope's Swiss Guard was reported to have changed from ceremonial garb to 'full war uniform'.

On page three the news shifted to the aftermath of the Allied victory in North Africa. I found an article about the first German and Italian prisoners of war sent to Fort Meade. They'd arrived yesterday – 1,632 Italians and 58 Germans.

Fort Meade was one of the first POW camps ready to accept Axis prisoners of war. The base was situated halfway between Washington and Baltimore just off Highway Fifty, less than an hour's drive away from Washington DC if one drove at the government-mandated speed limit of thirty-five miles per hour.

The article went on to say that Fort Meade had been a holding center for German-American internees, who were sent to other camps to make room for the prisoners of war.

My stomach clutched. German-American internees! Ada's

fears weren't exaggerated. I couldn't imagine her living behind a barbed wire fence. It would be a nightmare for her.

My bus braked to a stop at a renovated apartment house on 'E' Street. The building housed the Research and Analysis branch and the Registry of the Office of Strategic Services, where I had worked since early 1942. My job was often tedious, interrupted occasionally by an interesting assignment, but it was important. Better yet it paid well, and for the first time in my life I was independent. I had no intention of giving that freedom up, even if I had to file and type the rest of my life. Anything to avoid going back to Wilmington, North Carolina, to work at my parents' fish camp. I'd fried up enough fish and hushpuppies to last a lifetime already. But perhaps I didn't need to worry so much about that anymore. A couple of girls I knew passed by my window and I waved at them, trying to keep the glee and delight off my face. The bus jolted forward, and I remained in my seat.

This was the first day of my new job. I'd been promised more challenging work when Major Angus Wicker, whom I had met during a special assignment a few months ago, recruited me for a new OSS branch. I intended to learn new skills there that might help me stay employed after the war, when most of us government girls would lose our jobs.

The bus moved south and halted at the corner of 23rd and Constitution near the southern gate of the OSS complex.

I hopped off the bus and walked the few steps to the gate, showed my OSS ID to the guard and entered the compound. My new office was in Que building, immediately to the right of me, in one of the wooden 'tempos' built on the grounds of the compound.

Tempos were the temporary buildings thrown up quickly to house our rapidly expanding government. Roosevelt had ordered that they be built so poorly that they'd be quickly demolished once the war was over. World War I tempos had remained on the National Mall and surrounding the Reflecting Pool for years after that war ended and Roosevelt didn't want that to happen again. I didn't look forward to working in a tempo, but I sure was pleased with the move otherwise.

I'd been reassigned to the Morale Operations branch of

OSS. I wasn't sure of my job description. Major Wicker had been reticent when he offered me the position, but he had assured me it wouldn't be just clerical.

I opened the door to the building, noticing a half-inch gap between the doorframe and the door itself. In the winter this place would be cold. I almost collided with a spare woman in a trim navy blue suit, white blouse and neatly knotted white-and-blue-striped bow tie, who was waiting at the door. She grabbed my hand and pumped it firmly.

'I saw you get off the bus,' she said. 'You are Louise Pearlie, aren't you?'

'Yes, ma'am,' I said.

The woman radiated confidence and authority. She wasn't old, but she wasn't young either. A few grey hairs streaked through her dark hair, which was pulled back into a strict knot at her neck. She wore thick round eyeglasses similar to my own and no makeup, not even lipstick.

'I'm Miss Alice Osborne,' she said, slipping her arm into mine and propelling me forward. 'I see you're in civvies. Thank God you're not in the military. Some days this place looks like an army base.'

Miss Osborne led me through a madhouse masquerading as a large workroom. Art supplies, typewriters and desk lamps crowded several long wooden tables. German and Italian posters, newspapers, pamphlets and letters wallpapered the room, fastened with common nails hammered deeply into the wooden walls. One poster displayed the German alphabet in the antiquated style preferred by Adolf Hitler. Another was an artist's color wheel. Pencils lay scattered on the floor where they'd rolled off the tables and remained where they fell.

'Most of our artists work here,' Miss Osborne said. 'They design our "black" propaganda materials. They must be realistic and completely believable,' she said. 'Our agents in Europe send us as many samples of authentic German printed materials as they can.' There must have been twenty people, mostly men, crammed into the workroom, intent on their projects. None of them looked up at us as we walked through the space.

Black propaganda. I knew the Morale Operations branch

had been organized to distribute fake news, demoralizing rumors and forged printed materials to enemy soldiers and citizens. I was eager to know what work I would do here. I didn't know any foreign languages except a little French, and I wasn't one bit artistic.

Once through the workroom we entered a long narrow hall with doors ranging down its length on both sides. Halfway down the hall Miss Osborne flung a door open.

'This is your office,' she said to me, standing aside so I could enter.

There must be some mistake, I thought. This was a real office – well, all right, a closet. Crammed into it were a desk and chair, a file cabinet and a new Remington Rand typewriter on a dented metal cart. It looked like the office was all mine. No trying to concentrate with someone smoking or slurping coffee at my elbow! It had no windows, but that was a small price to pay for privacy.

'Here,' Miss Osborne said, thrusting a thick bound manual toward me. 'Read this. I don't have time to start training you yet, I've got to go to a meeting. I'll check back with you later.'

She closed the door behind her, leaving me standing behind my new desk feeling like a whirlwind had dropped me there. Before I could sit down the door opened again.

'Miss Pearlie,' Miss Osborne began.

'Mrs,' I said.

'Mrs Pearlie, did I tell you officially that you are my assistant?'

'No, ma'am,' I said.

'My office is right next door,' she said, nodding at the wall my desk faced. 'If you hear me knock on the wall come on over. I'll arrange for you to meet the staff later.' As the door closed behind her she said, in a muffled tone I could barely hear, 'You study that manual.'

The door opened again immediately and Miss Osborne leaned in, gripping the doorframe for support.

'If you want coffee the nearest coffee station is further down this hall in the anteroom to the general conference room,' she said. 'Sometimes people bring food.'

Then she was gone again. I still stood, waiting, and when I decided she wasn't going to pop back in I sat down to start my new job.

I wondered who exactly my new supervisor was. I knew her name, but not her title. For that matter I wondered what my title was, what exactly I would be doing and how much I would be paid. Would it be more than I was getting at the Registry? There was no sound coming from Miss Osborne's office next door. I wondered when I would see her again.

Opening the manual to the title page I read 'Morale Operations Field Manual'. I skimmed the first few pages of the guide. Just a few months old, MO was charged with spreading 'black' propaganda throughout the Mediterranean and Pacific theaters of war. MO's mission was to spread false rumors, false news reports, fake pamphlets and anything else that would demoralize the enemy. Bribery, blackmail and forgery were MO's most powerful tools. I was aware of MO because most of the OSS staff at the Research and Analysis branch complained when General Donovan first announced its formation. The academics who worked at R&A firmly believed that the United States should be above such nasty, ungentlemanly behavior. They insisted that information transmitted to German soldiers and citizens should be absolutely factual, 'white' propaganda. They weren't alone. A big percentage of the rest of OSS felt that American democracy could win the war using methods based on its ideals, not on the kinds of appalling psychological tactics used by the Nazis themselves.

But General Bill Donovan, Director of OSS, and President Roosevelt were men who believed 'the ends justified the means'. They were willing to do anything that would help us win the war. Anything.

My good friend Joan Adams, one of General Donovan's two secretaries, when she heard about my new assignment at lunch last week, seemed almost embarrassed. She ducked her head and leaned into me over her coffee.

'I mean,' she said, 'how are we different from the Nazis, if we behave just like them?'

I didn't say so, but I thought there was enough moral space between the United States and Nazi Germany that we could sacrifice some of that territory to win the war as quickly as possible. Before Europe was demolished and half its citizens cold in their graves.

I studied the glossary section of the manual first, which defined terms like *Mission*, *Task*, *Operative*, *Agent*, *Cutout* and such. I was familiar with most of them, except for *guerrillas*, which I had never heard before. *Guerrillas*, pronounced 'gorillas', were 'an organized band of individuals in enemy-held territory, indefinite as to number, which conducts against the enemy irregular operations of a military or quasi-military nature'. Whereas *Resistance Groups* focused on sabotage, espionage and non-cooperation. This wasn't a distinction I'd been aware of.

An hour later I'd read half the manual, pausing after the sections on bribery and blackmail. A headache gathered its strength, like a storm rising, at the back of my neck. I needed a cup of coffee and a couple of aspirin.

I ventured out of my closet office and down the narrow hallway, searching for the anteroom where the coffee was supposed to be. I came to the end of the building, past a dozen or so offices, and went around a corner. The coffee table sat outside the door of an occupied conference room. I could see the outlines of its inhabitants through the mottled glass window of the door and hear typewriters clacking, and even some arguing, as I made a beeline toward the coffee urn. A rangy man wearing scuffed cowboy boots and a leather belt with a big silver buckle moved away from his place leaning against the table.

'Good morning,' he said, in a Texas drawl. At least it sounded Texan to me. Not that I would know, except from Western movies. 'Who are you?' he asked.

'I'm Louise Pearlie,' I said. 'This is my first day here.'

'I'm Merle Ellison,' he said. He reached out a large hand and we shook. 'Call me Merle,' he said. 'Get yourself some coffee. There won't be a new pot until after lunch. I'm sorry though,' he said, nodding toward a crumby paper plate, 'I ate the last cookie.'

'That's OK,' I said. 'You don't know where I could find some aspirin, do you?'

Merle reached into his pocket and pulled out a tiny red tin of Bayer aspirin.

'Take two,' he said. I accepted, popping them into my throat and washing them down with coffee. 'So, what are you going to be doing here?' he asked.

'I don't really know,' I answered. 'I'm working with Miss Osborne, but I don't know what her title is or anything. She hasn't had time to talk with me yet. I'm reading the MO manual right now. What do you do here?'

'I'm a forger.'

The door to the conference room swung open, revealing a long table packed with people, mostly in uniform, mostly men, surrounded by coffee cups and mounds of paper. Like the workroom, its walls were plastered with maps, posters, German newspapers and other material I couldn't read from where I stood. Miss Osborne, who was sitting near the door, spotted me. She came out of the room and grabbed my arm.

'Good, you're here, she said. 'Come with me, I've got a job for you to do. Bring your coffee, if you like.'

I gestured a goodbye to Merle with my coffee cup and he nodded back, grinning.

Miss Osborne propelled me through an exterior door and guided me across a concrete pad to another tempo. We went inside and she took me into a small workroom furnished with a scarred wooden table and chair. Stacks of thick cardboard covered the table.

'We're cutting out stencils for our operatives in Germany to use to fake graffiti, see?' she said, picking up a completed stencil lettered in old-style German. She pointed to a sample sprayed directly on to the wall in black paint, revealing its message. 'It says "Will your son be the next to die?" We need another fifty of these. They need to be hand cut, or they won't look authentic. A little sloppiness is OK, it looks more natural.'

She handed me the master; the edges of its cut-out letters were razor sharp. 'Don't be so precise when you cut your letters. Like I said, the graffiti needs to look natural. And don't waste cardboard.'

'I'll be careful,' I said.

'You can take an hour lunch today, anytime between noon and one,' she said. 'I'll join you later and we'll pack these up.'

She went off without any further chitchat, leaving me by myself to cut the stencils.

I still didn't know Miss Osborne's title or my own, or if I would get a raise, but at least I wasn't typing index cards and filing in a room the size of an airplane hangar.

Cutting out the stencils was more difficult than I expected. I had to use both hands to force my scissors through the thick cardboard. My hands and forearms throbbed. After an hour I was only half done. I checked my watch. It was time for lunch. I was joining Joan at the OSS cafeteria. She'd want to know everything I felt comfortable telling her about my new job.

TWO

Joan had saved me a place in the cafeteria line just outside the door. A placard mounted on the wall nearby informed us that the special today was ham and macaroni bake. More pasta! If spaghetti and macaroni were ever rationed we would all fade away to nothing.

Joan bent down – she was quite tall – and pecked me on the cheek.

'I would kill for some beef,' she said, in her deep, throaty voice.

'I think they've got meatloaf,' I said.

'Not that! I want steak! I want to gnaw on the bone!' Joan had a hearty appetite, but she had plenty of money to buy good restaurant meals, if she wanted to. Her parents gave her an allowance of a hundred dollars a month to augment her OSS salary. She had a studio apartment in the Mayflower Hotel and a green Lincoln Continental cabriolet. It was a good thing I liked her so much or I'd have been consumed by envy.

We picked up our trays. I selected the macaroni and ham special with canned peas and corn. I detested Jell-O so I skipped the three colorful varieties offered and picked up an apple for dessert. Joan had the meatloaf after all and cherry Jell-O with canned grapes suspended inside.

We found seats for ourselves in a far corner of the cafeteria. It was crowded as always with a motley assortment of soldiers, spies, scholars and clerical staff, and the din allowed us to put our heads together and talk quietly. Here on the OSS campus we could speak more openly than we could outside its gates.

'How's the new job?' she asked.

'I don't know what I'm allowed to say about it. I haven't typed or filed all day. I have my own office, with a door and everything. Those are all encouraging. I'm somebody's assistant, but I don't know my title or my salary yet.'

'A new branch, it's bound to be a madhouse,' she said. 'Who is your boss?'

'I don't know if I can tell you,' I said. 'But madhouse is right.' I thought of the frantic workroom and the raised voices I heard behind the doors of the conference room.

'You're not going to tell me any more?' she asked.

'Joan, it's my first day. I don't know the lay of the land there yet. Let me settle in.'

Joan stirred her coffee. 'OK, OK. You are known for your reticence and I applaud you for it. What else is new with you?'

'Nothing much. You?'

'Me neither. I am working night and day.' Joan was an assistant to General Bill Donovan. He relied on her and she was intensely loyal to him.

'Have you heard from your Czech friend? Joe . . . was it Prager?' she asked.

Joe. I could feel the flush climbing up my neck and into my face at the mention of his name.

'You're still infatuated with him, obviously,' Joan said. 'You know you shouldn't be seeing him!'

Joan disapproved of Joe. He was a Czech refugee who traveled on a British passport. He worked, secretly, for a Jewish refugee organization, the Joint Distribution Committee, which helped Jews escape from Europe and settle into new lives wherever they could find a country that would admit them. Once Germany declared war on the United States, the JDC became a covert organization. Supposedly Joe taught Slavic languages at George Washington University. I had suspected his university job was a cover story a year ago when I discovered that his glasses had plain glass in their frames. So what did I do? I went to his department at GWU to ask him to join me for lunch. The receptionist had never heard of him. The next morning I followed him to an anonymous row house near campus. Cornered, he had to tell me the truth.

When I confronted Joe he insisted that his work was charitable and that he posed as a language professor only to protect his Czech family. The truth was he could have an entirely different job, one not so benign, which is what Joan feared. He could even be a Communist. Many East European refugees were. Whatever Joe's work, I knew in my heart he was one of the good guys. He had a real academic background, he'd been teaching Slavic literature in London when the war broke out. He'd joined the battle against the Nazis just like the rest of us. Having secrets didn't disqualify him from my affections. Washington was full of men and women with secrets. I kept secrets too.

And I'd been attracted to Joe from the minute I'd met him, and he to me.

'You know how risky it is to be seen with a foreigner,' Joan said. 'If OSS finds out you could lose your Top Secret clearance.'

'I'm not dating him,' I said. No, I wasn't dating him exactly, I was shacking up with him! I'd sneaked up to New York, where Joe had a temporary assignment, for a few weekends over the summer. Joe had the use of a friend's apartment and lived alone, something almost impossible to do in overcrowded Washington. At last we had the privacy that was impossible to find while we lived at 'Two Trees' together. The first weekend I'd visited him I'd jumped into his bed with alacrity and without feeling a bit guilty. I didn't even think about marrying him. I didn't know him well enough. Before I came to Washington, the idea of having relations with a man outside of marriage would have shocked me profoundly.

It still amazed me how far I'd traveled from my conventional life in Wilmington, North Carolina, where such a thing as an affair would be unthinkable. Run out of town on a rail unacceptable. But away from the scrutiny of my family, neighbors and the Baptist church I found I could do what I wanted, even have an affair with someone I didn't intend to marry.

In fact I hadn't been to church since I arrived in Washington. At first I told myself that because of work I needed to rest on Sunday, but as the months went on I realized how liberating it was not to have a Southern Baptist congregation keeping its collective eye on me.

'Joe's coming back to Washington soon,' I said to Joan. 'His assignment in New York is finished.' Joe couldn't live at 'Two Trees' since Milt had returned home to stay. It was just as well; it was so difficult to live in the same house and not give away our longing for each other.

'Stay away from him, Louise,' Joan said. 'You really must.'

I'd tried, I really had. But I was crazy about him, so we simply had to be as circumspect as possible.

I spent over an hour after lunch finishing the stencil job. My right arm was sore from my shoulder to my wrist. I'd need to keep a bottle of aspirin in my desk if most of my workdays were like this one.

The door opened and Miss Osborne leaned in, a pose I was beginning to get used to.

'Done?' she asked

'Almost,' I said.

She wheeled a hand truck into the room. 'When you're done load the stencils up and come to the conference room. We need to pack them up.'

'OK,' I said.

She left without another word – until she opened the door again.

'I forgot to tell you,' she said. 'Bring the stencil master too.'

The door closed again.

I was getting used to her sudden appearances and disappearances.

Half an hour later I trundled the hand truck stacked with stencils into the conference room. Miss Osborne was waiting for me. A pile of canvas bags with drawstrings waited for us in a box on the floor.

'Put a stencil in each bag,' she said. 'We need to get these on the next airplane to London. We've got a new outpost there. They don't have most of their supplies yet, but these need to be distributed as soon as possible. They've got other materials to stuff in the bags there. If we get them to London quickly they can go out on the next RAF bombing run.'

'Why are we sending them the master?' I asked, grabbing a bag and inserting a stencil into it.

'They'll have enough staff soon to do this themselves,' Miss Osborne said.

It didn't take long for us to finish filling the canvas bags. Miss Osborne turned them over to a Negro messenger who was waiting to drive them to Bolling Field.

'Lester, don't cut yourself on the master,' Miss Osborne said to the messenger. 'The edges are quite sharp.'

'No, ma'am,' Lester said, piling the canvas bags on the hand truck.

'Do you think you can make the last airplane to London?' she asked him, glancing at her watch. 'It leaves at five.'

'Sure,' he said, 'I know a shortcut.'

'Oh,' she said, glancing over at me as if surprised to see me, 'Lester, this is Mrs Pearlie, my new assistant.'

I stretched out a hand to shake his. He gripped me with a calloused paw so large it engulfed mine.

'I feel for you, Mrs Pearlie,' Lester said, smiling widely despite missing several teeth. 'This woman, she be a slave driver! Works you all day long!'

'I haven't worn you out yet, have I?' Miss Osborne asked him.

'No, ma'am,' Lester said, wheeling the hand truck out of the conference room. 'But it would be nice to get a break sometime to smoke a cigarette!'

'That's one project finished,' Miss Osborne said, after Lester had closed the conference door behind him. 'Speaking of cigarettes, I need one. Haven't had a smoke since lunch.' She pulled her pocketbook off the back of her chair, where she'd slung it before we began to pack the bags. She rummaged around inside it for a minute before pulling out a pack of Lucky Strikes and a trench army lighter.

'Want one?' she asked.

'No, thanks, I don't smoke.'

She lit her cigarette and inhaled deeply. I could see her shoulders relax.

'Quite a day,' she said. 'Have you finished the MO field manual?'

'No, but I have just a few pages more.'

'Good,' she said. 'I've got something else you can get done before the end of the day.' She pulled a spiral composition book out of her pocketbook and handed it to me. 'Would you please type up the notes I took this morning?' she said.

'Of course,' I said, taking the notebook from her hand. 'I've got a typewriter, but no office supplies.'

'Damn,' she said, 'I forgot to requisition them.' Stubbing out her cigarette she rose from her seat and slung her pocketbook over her shoulder. 'Come to my office and I'll give you some to tide you over.'

Miss Osborne's office was only slightly larger than mine. There was a cot with a blanket and pillow neatly piled on top, so she must sleep here occasionally. I made a mental note to keep a toothbrush and spare undies in my handbag from now on.

Miss Osborne scrabbled around in her messy desk drawers and gathered typing paper, an eraser, carbon paper, pencils and a few file folders. She shoved them across the desk to me, then ripped a requisition form off a pad and scrawled an illegible signature across the bottom.

'Here,' she said, handing it to me. 'I've signed it, but you list what you need. You might want to go to the supply room in the morning and pick everything up; otherwise it could be a couple of days before your order's delivered.' Or much of it would be missing! The supply department had a habit of shorting every request for supplies to save money.

I seized on this brief moment when Miss Osborne wasn't in motion to ask her about my job.

'Ma'am,' I said, 'would you mind telling me what your title is, and mine? Do you know what my salary is?'

'Oh, hell's bells,' she said. 'No one told you? Of course. Have a seat.'

I sat down while she sorted through the folders on her desk.

'Here it is,' she said, opening a file. 'Our big boss is the Deputy Director of Psychological Warfare Operations. I'm the Administrative Assistant for the European Theater of Operations. Our branch chief is Lt Colonel Roller; I report to the deputy chief, Mr Baldwin.'

I had never heard of any of these men. They must be new to OSS.

'Let's see now,' she continued. 'Your title is Junior

Administrative Assistant, salary twenty-six hundred dollars. Does that sound right?'

'Yes, ma'am,' I said evenly, trying not to betray my delight. This was a definite promotion. And a six hundred dollar raise – fifty extra dollars a month! What was I going to do with all that money?

'I'm off to another meeting,' she said, slinging her bag over her shoulder. 'You can leave at five thirty today, if you wish.'

She was gone before I had a chance to respond.

Next door, in my own office, I sat at my typewriter for the first time. I wondered if I needed to make a carbon copy of the notes I was typing up. I decided to do so. I could always shred it if Miss Osborne wanted me to.

Slipping sheets of paper and carbon paper into my type-writer, I began to decipher her notes. Much of the manuscript was in shorthand. Miss Osborne must once have been an ordinary secretary. Thank goodness I remembered most of my shorthand from business school! What I couldn't remember I inferred. When I filled out my requisition form I'd include a copy of the Gregg shorthand manual.

My typed notes filled just two pages, single-spaced since the government needed to save paper. I filed my own copy and went next door to deposit one in Miss Osborne's inbox. Back in my own office I filled out the requisition form, listing everything I could possibly think of, even cellophane tape.

It was five thirty in the evening. Time to go home. I felt as though I had just arrived; the day had sped by. Instead of typing and filing without relief as my workday at the Registry crawled by, I'd actually had varied assignments. This was a definite improvement in my life. If I ever saw Major Wicker again I'd thank him again for his reference.

When I climbed on to my bus I saw a girl I knew from the Registry and sat down beside her.

'I heard that you got a new job,' she said. 'Do you like it?'

'I love it,' I answered.

*   *   *

As soon as my boarding house came into view my happiness with my new job dissipated. What was I going to tell Ada? The MO branch was on the other side of the OSS compound from the Registry and the vast collection of OSS files where I once toiled. How could I just waltz into the Registry and look for a list of German prisoners of war? It would arouse the suspicion of all my former co-workers and supervisors. It had nothing to do with my new job. I didn't even know if such a list existed! I'd stupidly tried to calm Ada's fears, but instead I'd raised her expectations of something I might not be able to do.

Stepping inside the dark foyer of 'Two Trees' I strained to hear Ada's voice. If she had a gig tonight maybe I could avoid a scene by leaving a note on her bed. What a coward I was! But it was Phoebe who greeted me, coming out of the lounge with her hands clasped and delight in her eyes.

'Louise!' she said. 'Guess who's here!'

'Who?' I asked, wondering if her second son was home on leave.

'Joe! He's going to have dinner with us tonight.'

My heart leapt and choked off my voice.

'Really?' I said squeakily. 'How nice.' The last letter I'd received from Joe had said he didn't know exactly when he'd be back in Washington.

Joe himself walked out of the lounge. I wanted to throw myself into his arms, but instead I stood rooted to the spot, folding my hands in front of me to keep them still. My ears pounded and the hallway receded from my vision as if I was going to faint. I reached for the newel post of the staircase to steady myself. Damn him for not letting me know he would be here! I felt exposed, afraid Phoebe and the other boarders would be able to read my vulnerability in my face.

Joe wasn't anyone's idea of a leading man. He had a medium build, dark hair and a dark beard and wore cheap metal-framed glasses. He dressed in well-worn suits that could easily have come from a thrift shop. He was rarely without his scuffed leather briefcase, pipe and a bag of Prince Albert tobacco. He was the picture of his cover story, a refugee college professor.

I was attracted to Joe in a way I had never been to any

other man. My first husband, Bill Pearlie, had been my best friend since childhood. I loved him, and I was devastated when he died, but it wasn't this heart-stopping, even dangerous, sort of emotion. Joe was more sophisticated than I. He'd lived in London and knew about opera, theatre and fine food. He had an adorable accent, lightly trilling his 'rs'. But despite his urbanity and education he never condescended to me.

As I clung to the staircase Joe broke my indecision about what to do by taking my arm and planting a brotherly kiss on my forehead.

'Louise,' he said, 'it's so good to see you!'

'And you,' I managed to say in my normal voice.

'Take off your hat and come into the lounge,' Phoebe said. 'We're celebrating! Joe brought us champagne.'

Milt and Henry stood up as I entered the lounge and I took a seat on the davenport. Joe took the spot next to me on the davenport and Phoebe took another chair.

'This room looks so attractive,' Joe said. 'What have you done with it?'

'Ada and Louise slipcovered the chairs and davenport for me. Didn't they do a nice job? I love the fabric,' Phoebe said.

I wouldn't have chosen the pink and green floral for myself but Ada and I knew Phoebe would love it. It had taken us many weekends to finish, but it was worth it to please Phoebe. We lived in relative luxury at 'Two Trees' and we knew it. In most other boarding houses we would be sharing our small bedrooms with roommates.

'Where is Ada?' I asked Phoebe.

'She's working,' Phoebe said. 'At a private reception at the Statler.'

Milt handed me a glass of champagne and I gulped the first swallow. I needed to steady myself. The shock of seeing Joe had worn off, but still I had to pretend I was no more than his friend.

'Joe was telling us where he's living now,' Henry said. 'You know that huge block of apartments between Virginia Avenue and New Hampshire?'

'You mean the Potomac Plaza?' I said.

'That's the one,' Joe said. 'It's not much to look at but it's not far from George Washington.' He meant the university where Phoebe and the rest of the boarders thought he taught. Except he didn't.

'You're going back to work there again?' Milt asked.

'Yes,' Joe said, 'I'll be teaching Slavic languages to classes full of soldiers, like before.'

'I don't understand why you went to New York in the first place,' Henry said.

Joe shrugged. 'I expound on diacritical marks wherever I'm sent,' he said. 'I don't ask questions.'

'Thank God,' Joe said, when Dellaphine, our cook and housekeeper, brought in an immense platter of fried chicken and set it on the dining room table in front of Phoebe. 'I've missed your cooking,' he said to her.

Dellaphine beamed at him. She had a soft spot for Joe.

'I've fixed the mashed potatoes just the way you like them,' she said.

'A little lumpy,' Henry said under his breath.

If Dellaphine had heard him she wouldn't have cared. Henry was not her favorite boarder.

She left the dining room and came back with bowls of mashed potatoes and butterbeans and a basket of homemade yeast rolls. I was disappointed we only had margarine to melt over it all. I'd thought we had most of our butter ration left.

Phoebe served the chicken, giving Joe both a breast and a drumstick, I noticed. She scooped up a heap of already sliced chicken from the platter and served her son. Milt wouldn't let us help him at the table. If his food needed to be cut up Dellaphine or Phoebe did it in the kitchen. Once our plates were full of chicken we passed the side dishes around and focused on eating.

'I'm sorry I took your bed,' Milt said to Joe. 'It wasn't part of my plan to come home before the war ended.'

'It's OK,' Joe said. 'The apartment is fine. I'm sharing it with a friend. It's a two and a half roomer.' So the apartment had a kitchen, living room and one bedroom. So much for privacy, I thought. We couldn't be together unless we rented a hotel room, and I just wouldn't do that. Someone might report our 'tryst' to the FBI, since conscientious Washingtonians wouldn't hesitate to notice an unmarried couple, one of whom had an eastern European accent, shacked up in a hotel room. I could lose my security clearance. And I didn't know what Phoebe would do if she found out I was with Joe instead of out of town. Even Ada came home every night, even if it was three o'clock in the morning. When I went to New York to visit Joe I pretended I was spending a weekend at a guest-house in Maryland on the Chesapeake Bay. Phoebe was a wonderful person but she was a traditional Southern lady. If she found out I was having an affair with Joe she might evict me.

'But,' Joe said, without looking at me, 'my roommate's gone most weekends. His family lives in Virginia, in Manassas. He visits them as often as he can.'

Joe's words gave me hope that we could spend time together, and I felt a flush climb up my neck. I willed it to stop, and held my glass of cold milk to my face. I thought I must be bright red, but nobody seemed to notice.

We cleaned up every morsel of our dinner.

'My turn,' I said, getting out of my seat to help Dellaphine clear the table. The word 'turn' meant either Phoebe or me. The men kept their seats.

In the kitchen I said hello to Madeleine, Dellaphine's twenty-year-old daughter. She helloed back at me. She was still dressed in the neat suit that she'd worn to her clerical job at the Social Security Administration. She'd already washed the pots and pans – as shown by the stack on the drain board end of the big sink – and was back sitting at the kitchen table, turning the pages of the *Negro Digest*.

I stacked the dishes in the sink while Dellaphine ducked into the pantry. She came out beaming, carrying a beautiful iced chocolate cake on a serving plate.

'Miss Phoebe told me Mr Joe would be here in time for me to bake his favorite cake,' she said.

'Is that where the last of the butter and sugar went?' I asked.

'Sure is,' she answered. 'I don't think anyone will mind.'

'I'm sure no one will,' I said, my mouth already watering just thinking about buttercream frosting.

'Why don't you take it in?' she said. 'I'll get started on the dishes.'

Everyone at the table murmured happily when I presented the cake. Milt picked up his fork in anticipation before Phoebe cut the first slice.

I took the first two pieces Phoebe sliced back into the kitchen for Dellaphine and Madeleine. Mine was waiting at my place when I returned to the table. It was delicious, a real cake at a time when we often had to settle for canned fruit.

Joe went back into the kitchen and thanked Dellaphine for the cake, then joined us in the lounge. There was a little champagne left, and Phoebe divided it up into our champagne glasses so we could each have another swallow.

'Do you mind listening to the radio?' Henry asked. 'Bing Crosby's on.'

I'd heard enough of Bing Crosby to last me a lifetime, but I couldn't complain as long as my fellow boarders allowed me to listen to the Grand Ole Opry on Saturday nights.

Joe and I sat beside each other on the davenport. The hair on my arms prickled when I felt his hand rest next to mine while we listened to Bing croon. It was a struggle not to lay my head on his shoulder.

The program ended and Joe stirred. He turned to me.

'Do you know if the Western Market is still open?' he asked. 'I need to pick up some groceries.'

'You've got thirty minutes,' I said.

'I'd better be off, then,' he said.

After hugs from Phoebe and me and firm handshakes from Henry and Milt, Joe left.

I slipped into the kitchen where Madeleine and Dellaphine were drinking after dinner coffee.

'I'm going to feed the chickens and check on the garden,' I said to them.

On the back stoop I filled a bucket with corn and almost ran to the chicken coop in the backyard. Dumping the corn in the coop and the bucket on the ground I went around the house to the front, opened the gate, walked quickly down the street and met Joe in front of the Western Market.

Out in the open we didn't dare embrace. Instead I whacked him on the arm. 'Why didn't you call me and tell me you were in town?' I asked. 'I could have blown everything.'

Joe rubbed his arm. 'I'm sorry,' he said. 'I couldn't call you at work, could I? When I arrived at Union Station I called my friend who'd offered to share his apartment with me. Then I thought I should call Phoebe to give you some kind of heads-up. She invited me to dinner and I couldn't think of a reason to decline. So I just showed up. I knew you could handle it.'

'I thought you weren't sure when you were coming back to town.'

'I got my instructions this morning, with barely enough time to pack and catch the train. Sorry I surprised you.'

'I forgive you,' I said. 'I'm so glad you're here.'

He glanced up and down the empty street.

'Anyone could be looking out of the windows,' I said.

'I'll be in touch when I can,' he said.

'When your roommate is out of town,' I answered.

'Yes. I'd better get on to the market,' he said.

Our arms hung at our sides. I'd wanted desperately for him to move back to DC, but this was difficult. Almost worse than being apart.

'So long,' I said.

'Bye.'

I was the first to turn, walking quickly back to 'Two Trees'. Letting myself into the backyard through a side gate, I grabbed a couple of late tomatoes and some butternut squash from the garden and climbed the back steps to the kitchen. Thankfully no one was there to see me arrive, breathing hard and flustered. I dumped the vegetables on the drain board and walked quietly down the hall toward the staircase. I wanted to be alone. I heard the radio in the lounge but no voices.

I tiptoed up the stairs and went into my room, throwing myself on the bed, my heart pounding. I waited for it to slow down before I went into the bathroom I shared with Phoebe and Ada to wash up. Since it was Ada's day for a full bath I just sponged off in the sink.

Back in my bedroom I changed into my pajamas and climbed into my bed. It was still early, but what a day I had had! It felt like midnight. I picked up Lloyd Douglas's new bestseller *The Robe* but fell sound asleep before I came to the end of the chapter.

Lying on his bunk in his tent in the dark, waiting for reveille to sound, Thomas Hanzi couldn't believe his good fortune. From the moment he'd marched off the crowded Liberty Ship *Abel Stoddard* on to the dock in Baltimore Harbor he'd felt like he was living in a dream.

What a place America was! The German press had described the country as a ruin, bombed almost into submission by the Luftwaffe, but there was no sign of damage or suffering anywhere. Well-dressed people carrying shopping bags or briefcases walked quickly, with purpose, in the streets of Baltimore. Once his train moved into the lush green countryside he saw fields thick with bales of harvested hay and fat cows. In Germany soldiers had ridden in cattle cars, sometimes for days on end, eating canned meat and hard crackers for each meal. Here the prisoners traveled in passenger compartments and ate fresh sandwiches layered with real meat and cheese and fruit for lunch. The bread on their sandwiches was white! He was accustomed to black bread that had to be soaked in coffee before he could chew it.

Most astounding to him were the colored people. He'd been told that all colored people were slaves in America. But the army sergeant who'd marched his column of prisoners of war from the Baltimore dock to the train station was a colored man! And so was the train conductor! In Germany this would be unthinkable. Thomas was a gypsy, and he was well aware that only his blue eyes had kept him from being sent to a forced labor camp years ago. Not that he was much better off in the Wehrmacht. He had dug ditches in the sand and dirt under a broiling sun for an engineering squad in Tunisia. He'd worked in sand, slept in sand, his clothes were full of it and it seasoned the sausage stew he ate for midday dinner, the only hot meal he received during the day.

When he arrived at the American camp for German prisoners

of war Hanzi was assigned to a tent with just three other people. The cots had mattresses and blankets. Every meal was hot and included vegetables and dessert. His German money had been converted to credits at the camp PX, where he could buy beer after dinner! And he had a free daily ration of cigarettes and candy.

As a child he'd detested, loathed the man, whoever he was, who had given him his blue eyes. But as the Nazis gained control of Germany his eyes became his salvation. Himmler classified a few Roma gypsies as acceptable – part-Aryan, so to speak. Someone had to collect the garbage. So Hanzi watched his dark-eyed friends and family disappear, but the little bit of Aryan blood he had meant he was allowed to sweep streets and keep his caravan in Marzahn, the open field outside Berlin, a gypsy ghetto where those of his people still left were forced to live, until he was conscripted into the army to dig ditches and latrines.

In America he was treated no differently than any other prisoner of war by his captors. But he wasn't a fool. He knew he wasn't completely safe. His fellow prisoner Obersturmführer Steiner was a Nazi, Waffen SS; he despised Hanzi for his gypsy blood, he could see it every time he caught Steiner staring at him. Steiner would kill him if he could find a way.

He was also careful to stay far away from Sturmbannführer Kapp. He often found this SS major staring at him too, but in an odd way, not with hate, like Steiner, but with a look he didn't understand or like. Hanzi and his people had always survived by avoiding attention, and that would remain his strategy unless he was backed into a corner.

The camp speakers played reveille, and someone turned on the light in his tent. But instead of jumping up to dress so he could go to the mess for coffee and breakfast, Hanzi started to moan like a man in pain. Right above his head, so close that it almost touched him, dangled a noose.

Hanzi was so terrified he couldn't move, his eyes fixed on the noose, and kept moaning until that kind Leutnant Bahnsen grabbed him under the armpits and dragged him off his cot and out of the tent.

THREE

I was awake so early the next morning that I ate in the kitchen with Madeleine instead of waiting for the others to come downstairs. Dellaphine fixed us fluffy scrambled eggs, courtesy of our own chickens, with a strip of bacon and plenty of toast each. Madeleine ate quickly, smearing a teaspoon of strawberry jam on her second piece of toast, then got to her feet, throwing her pocketbook over her shoulder and pushing her straightened shoulder-length hair back from her face. Dellaphine frowned at her.

'You finish eating at the table,' she said to Madeleine.

'I don't want to miss my bus,' she said. 'And, Momma, I won't be home for dinner. Some of us girls are going to eat at the YMCA cafeteria and go see *Stormy Weather*.'

'What's that?' Dellaphine asked.

'It's a new movie,' Madeleine said. 'With Bill Robinson and Lena Horne.'

'You know how I feel about you going out on a weeknight,' Dellaphine said.

'I'm not in high school anymore, Momma. I'll be back by ten o'clock, I promise,' Madeleine said, waving her hand goodbye to us as she went out the back door.

'That girl,' Dellaphine said. 'If I got up from the table before I was finished eating my momma would rap me on the knuckles.'

'She didn't want to miss her bus,' I said. I felt for Madeleine. She was an adult with a good job but had to share a room in the basement with her mother. She couldn't get decent housing anywhere else because she was colored.

Dellaphine set her mouth and added more bacon to her skillet.

I heard the telephone in the hall ring and Phoebe's voice answer it. A minute later she appeared at the kitchen door, still wearing her dressing gown, her hair fastened in pin curls with bobby pins.

'It's for you,' she said to me. 'It's a woman.'

Thinking it might be my mother, wondering if there was an emergency of some kind at home in Wilmington, I hurried down the hall to the phone and picked up the receiver.

'Mrs Pearlie, it's Miss Osborne,' said the voice on the other end of the line.

'Yes, ma'am,' I said, wondering what on earth she was calling me about at home so early in the morning.

'You and I are going out of town today,' she said. 'Bring your suitcase, be prepared to stay overnight for a couple of days. Meet me in the conference room at nine.'

I had my mouth open to ask her to explain, but she hung up before I could get a question out, leaving me staring at the receiver.

'Is everything all right?' Phoebe asked. She paused at the foot of the staircase with her cup of coffee in her hand. She would take it upstairs to drink while she dressed and wouldn't come downstairs again until she was fully clothed and made up, ready for the day.

'I'm going out of town on business,' I said. 'I'll be gone overnight for several days.'

Phoebe looked incredulous. 'What next?' she asked. 'In my day no single woman would do such a thing!'

'I need to pack a bag and catch an early bus.' I had to pick up my office supplies before I met Miss Osborne so I would have what I needed to do my work.

I followed Phoebe upstairs. She was still shaking her head as we parted in the hall. I pulled my late husband's scarred leather valise out of my closet and threw in enough underwear for three days, and my pajamas and robe. I chose a felt fedora to wear instead of my summer straw. It looked more business-like. Then I selected another dress to take so I could change at least once, and a cardigan sweater in case the weather cooled. I wondered where on earth Miss Osborne and I were going. I figured that I'd need my largest handbag to carry a notebook and paperwork, so I dug out my square black leather bag with the wide opening.

I sat down to write a note to Ada, explaining that I hadn't yet found a way of getting a list of the German prisoners of war arriving in the States. I gathered up my valise, handbag and the note and left my room. Pausing outside Ada's door, I listened carefully. I didn't hear anything, so I slipped the note under her door. *Coward*, I said to myself.

At the OSS supply depot, inside another tempo built on top of a stone patio deep inside the OSS compound, the private on duty filled a file box with everything I'd requested, including a used copy of the Gregg shorthand manual.

'Can you carry this OK?' the private asked, nodding at the valise at my feet. 'That's a lot of weight for a girl. Can I call a porter for you?'

'No, thanks,' I said, 'I'll be fine.' Shoving the narrow handle of my valise over my wrist and throwing my handbag strap over my shoulder, I picked up the file box and strode confidently out the door.

Halfway back to the Morale branch tempo I had to stop and catch my breath. The box and valise weren't heavy, but carrying them was clumsy. I had to lean to the side to keep my balance with the valise while hanging on to the corners of the box, which cut into my forearms. I didn't want to fall and make a fool of myself, but I didn't want to call a porter either. It might get back to the annoying private at the supply depot.

Help arrived in the person of Merle, who appeared at my side carrying a cardboard suitcase tied shut with rope. Merle must be going out of town too. He raised an eyebrow at the sight of my valise, but of course we couldn't ask each other questions out in the open, even in the OSS compound.

'Let me help you,' Merle said. 'Give me your valise and I'll carry it to your office.'

'Thanks,' I said, relieved I wouldn't have to call for a porter.

Merle dropped my valise on the floor behind my door while I set the box of supplies on my desk. I rummaged around in the box and found a stenographer's notebook, a couple of pencils and a bottle of ink for my fountain pen. I shoved everything into my handbag.

'Well,' Merle said, still gripping his own suitcase, 'we're both leaving town, obviously. I'm going for work. You?'

'Me too,' I said. 'Where are you headed?'

'I don't know yet,' he answered.

'Me either,' I said.

'Do you have a meeting at nine this morning with Miss Osborne?'

'I do! Do you think we're going on the same trip?'

'I guess we'll find out soon enough.' Merle checked his watch. 'We've got enough time to leave my suitcase in my office and get a cup of coffee before we're due at the conference room.'

'Sounds good,' I said.

Merle's office was a bit larger than mine, holding a drafting table set under the only window and a tall stool instead of the usual desk and chair. A battered metal cabinet on wheels crammed with art supplies stood within reach of the table. A rickety set of shelves held stacks of paper of all kinds. What seemed to be genuine personal letters written in German, with German postmarks and stamps, were nailed to the wall over his drafting table. A gooseneck lamp was angled over the table, where I could see that he was working on a project.

'We have a few minutes,' Merle said. 'Want to see some of my work?'

'I'd like to very much,' I said.

'I'm writing a personal letter from a fictional soldier,' Merle said, showing me the half-written letter, ornate fountain pen and ink bottle labeled in German on his drafting table. 'Of course,' he said, 'the pen, ink and paper are all authentic. Bought or stolen for us by our agents in Europe.' He nodded in the direction of the German alphabet posters fastened to his wall. 'I use those as examples. The Germans use several alphabets, and sometimes they mix up the letters in one document.'

Merle's letter looked damned authentic to me. 'What does it say?' I asked.

'The gist of it is it's a letter from a soldier to his mother, complaining that German officers have better food than the enlisted men, that hundreds of young German men are dying every day and that he's terrified he'll be next. OSS London will get the letter to a resistance agent in Germany, who will plant it somewhere German civilians are likely to pick it up, like a train station or a bar. They'll feel less confidence in the Reich and the progress of the war.'

I was impressed by Merle's forgery, and I wondered about his background. He might look like a cowboy, but the man was an artist.

'What did you do before the war?' I asked.

'I was an illustrator for the *Amarillo Daily News*,' he said. 'My parents own a small ranch, but I didn't want to spend my life mucking out stables.'

I checked my watch. 'We'd better go,' I said. 'We don't want to be late.'

We poured ourselves cups of black coffee on our way to the conference room. What sugar and milk had been there first thing in the morning was already gone.

Miss Osborne and a man in a khaki naval ensign's uniform, with a single bar and star on the sleeves and shoulder epaulets, were already seated at the conference table.

'Don't take any notes,' Miss Osborne said to me before I even sat down. 'This is ears only. Mr Ellison, Mrs Pearlie, this is Ensign David Winton, the Executive Officer of MO branch.'

Ensign Winton half rose from his seat and shook our hands. He didn't look like a naval ensign to me, or how I expected a junior naval officer to look. He was some years older than me, maybe forty. He had thinning light brown hair and a slight, unfit body. Surely his glasses were too thick for the military. But then I realized that the naval commission was part of the effort to militarize the OSS. I'd had some pressure to join the WACs myself, but I excused myself on the basis of being too old and jaded to live with a bunch of nineteen-year-old women. And I didn't want the pay cut, to live in a barracks or get ordered around any more than I was already. Which sounded so unpatriotic that I kept it to myself.

'I don't have much time,' Winton said, taking his seat again. 'I'm due at General Donovan's office in half an hour.'

'OK,' Miss Osborne said. She turned to Merle and me. 'You are both familiar with "*Wie Lange Noch?*", the "How Much Longer?" propaganda campaign? Mrs Pearlie, you may not recognize the title, but the stencils you cut yesterday are part of it. And of course, Mr Ellison, your forged letters. It's our first complex "black" campaign, designed to demoralize the German people.'

'General Donovan is pleased with the operation so far,' Winton said. 'The materials you've generated have been excellent. Our problem is that we have few people to distribute them. We've invented a German resistance group to take credit for the operation, but the materials still need to be distributed.'

'There are very few actual German resistance members,' Miss Osborne said to us, 'which I'm sure doesn't surprise you. So we plan to recruit operatives to deliver much of this material in northern Italy behind German lines.'

Winton paused to take a cigarette out of a battered pack of unfiltered Marlboros and offered the pack to us. Merle and I refused, but Miss Osborne took one and lit it from the match Winton offered her. Both of them inhaled deeply.

'You know that the Germans are putting up a real fight in Italy,' Winton said. 'The Italian surrender hasn't discouraged them one bit. We think, and OSS London agrees, that because of the chaos there, and because of a sympathetic population, if we deliver our propaganda behind German lines in northern Italy, much of it will find its way into Germany.'

'But we need people to deliver it,' Miss Osborne said. 'Native Germans who look and sound like they belong wherever our subs out of Malta can drop them off.'

Winton crushed out his cigarette in one of the metal ashtrays on the table. 'I need to go. But I wanted to be here for a few minutes this morning to emphasize to you how important this mission is. Miss Osborne will finish briefing you.'

I hoped so. I didn't have the faintest idea what mission Winton was talking about, or what we were supposed to do. Short of landing in Italy ourselves and nailing posters to trees I had no idea.

After Winton left Miss Osborne stubbed out her cigarette and leaned over the table toward us. 'You know one of the first groups of German and Italian prisoners of war has arrived in the United States,' she said. 'We want to recruit German POWs to go back into northern Italy and distribute our propaganda materials. They'll be able to penetrate further into the German lines than the Italians. It's our job to interrogate these prisoners of war to see whom we might be able to trust. The Nazis will be tough nuts to crack, but not all of the captured Germans are Nazis. Some of them are just soldiers, many of them drafted. Soldiers who might be willing to work with us to bring the war to an early end. I'll be conducting the interviews with the German POWs at Fort Meade and you will assist me. When we've identified and trained our recruits we'll send them to Malta to begin the operation. But there's not much point in generating propaganda material until we have operatives to deliver it. We've got to recruit them right away.'

'Miss Osborne, I don't speak German,' I said.

'Neither do I,' she said.

'Will Fort Meade provide a translator?'

'Mr Ellison will be translating for us.'

I shifted in my seat and looked at Merle. I already knew that Merle could read and write German, because he was forging a letter in German, but speaking it fluently was an altogether different matter.

'I'm third-generation,' Merle said. 'My grandparents never learned English, so to talk with them I had to speak German. I'm fluent, but I speak with a powerful Texas accent. I couldn't pass for a native German if my life depended on it.'

'OK, are you two ready to go?' she asked. 'The car is probably already waiting for us at the gate.'

Lester tossed our bags in the back of an open jeep. All but one, which Miss Osborne grabbed back from him and kept with her. To me it looked suspiciously like an OSS suitcase radio. Miss Osborne saw me staring at it, wondering if we were going to set up a covert radio somewhere. 'It's a tape recorder,' she said. 'We'll be recording all our interviews.'

She took the passenger seat while Merle and I clambered into the narrow back seat. We held on to our hats as the jeep pulled out on to Constitution Avenue and accelerated.

I leaned forward to speak to Miss Osborne, still holding on to my hat with one hand.

'Ma'am,' I said, 'could we ask Lester to stop long enough to put up the jeep top? We're getting blown away back here.'

'The airfield isn't far,' she answered. 'We'll be there before you know it.'

'The airfield?'

'Didn't I tell you? We're hitching a ride on a military transport flight to Fort Meade.'

I felt my stomach churn as I leaned back in my seat. I had never been on an airplane before! I couldn't imagine what it would feel like to be up in the air so high. It gave me the heebie-jeebies just to climb into the steeple of my church back home.

I kept a firm grip on my hat as we traveled east, skirting the Capitol and then turning southeast on Pennsylvania Avenue. Well before entering Maryland we turned even further south, to the eastern shore of the Potomac, and drew up to the gates of the Naval Air Station.

The navy MP on duty at the gate raised his hand to halt us, but after a quick examination of Miss Osborne's papers he motioned us through the gate and into the airfield. Our jeep pulled right up to a two-engine military transport plane parked on a dirt runway. My nerves began to overwhelm me. Why were we flying to Fort Meade instead of driving? The base was only thirty-five miles or so from Washington! We could drive it in an hour! Of course, I reminded myself, with wartime traffic it could be much longer.

I wished I didn't have a new, exciting job. I'd give anything to be wandering among the forest of file cabinets at the Registry just now.

Merle noticed the fear in my eyes as he helped me out of the jeep. He leaned over and whispered in my ear. 'It'll be OK, it's a real short flight to Fort Meade. Maybe a half-hour, depending on air traffic.'

'What if I heave?' I whispered back. Merle opened his jacket to show me the brown paper bags he'd tucked into his pocket. 'I brought these. You wouldn't be the first to use one.'

Lester carried our bags over to the belly of the plane and stowed them in the storage compartment. A navy seaman, looking quite odd on an airfield, latched the door.

I followed Miss Osborne as she climbed the movable metal staircase into the airplane. Inside quarters were so close that Merle had to duck his head. Eight seats, four on each side of a narrow aisle, crowded the claustrophobic passenger compartment. A sliding panel at the front of the plane concealed the cockpit. There were two flyboys up there, thank God. If one of them had an appendicitis attack the other one could land the airplane.

I edged down the aisle and scrunched myself into the seat behind Miss Osborne, buckling my safety belt, pulling it as tight as I could tolerate. She turned her head to speak to me.

'Mrs Pearlie,' she said, 'have you ever flown before?'

'No, ma'am,' I said, trying to sound nonchalant.

'You'll love it,' she said. 'Everything looks amazing from up in the sky, and you get where you're going so quickly, and it's less tiring than driving.'

'I'm sure,' I said.

'This is an Electra 10, although the navy calls it something else,' Miss Osborne added. 'It's basically the same airplane Amelia Earhart flew. I don't think they'll ever find her, do you?'

'No, ma'am,' I said. So here I was, trapped inside a big cigar tube with a half-inch of metal and rivets between me and the open air, about to fly off and away into the blue sky, something no human being other than Superman was meant to do. If Amelia Earhart had crashed in one of these airplanes were any of us safe? It was only by sheer willpower that I didn't unlatch my seatbelt and run screaming down the aisle and beat on the exit door.

Merle must have noticed my hand gripping my armrest so tightly that my knuckles were white. He reached across the aisle and grasped my wrist, squeezing it reassuringly. Then he passed me a brown bag. I stuffed it into my handbag.

The two propellers engaged, and the Pratt & Whitney engines roared with increasing volume. Looking out my window I could see the propeller on my side of the plane rotate more and more quickly until it blurred. The aircraft actually trembled and rattled with a metallic sound. Was it supposed to do that? No one seemed troubled but me, and that included the three officers seated at the front of the plane. Two army light colonels and a navy captain, I could tell by the bars on their sleeves, on their way to Fort Meade for some reason. One of the colonels was calm enough to be asleep already!

Our version of Amelia Earhart's plane turned and headed down the dirt airstrip. We lifted into the air, and I felt as well as heard a huge thud beneath my feet. My stomach stayed behind on the ground but I managed not to barf.

'What was that noise?' I shouted to Merle over the sound of the engines.

He leaned toward me. 'The wheels retracting,' he shouted back. 'They'll make a racket when we prepare to land too.'

I kept my eye on the horizon while clutching my bag with both hands as if I expected someone to try to take it from me. Beneath me the dirt runway of the airstrip receded as we headed north toward Maryland. The Capitol, gleaming white marble in the midst of a hodgepodge of tacky tempos, passed to my left far below. I guessed we were well short of the aircraft's cruising altitude, but it was still too high for me. We followed Route 1 into Maryland, and I thought I could see Baltimore in the distance when the airplane shuddered again.

'It's just the wing flaps,' Merle shouted into my ear. 'We'll be landing soon.'

Fort Meade stretched out below us. I spotted neat rows of brick barracks, a small church and a vehicle depot full of trucks and jeeps. A column of tiny men marched across a parade ground. Further north row upon row of white tents stood behind a tall barbed wire fence cornered by watchtowers.

We landed on a dirt airstrip half the size of the one we had left in Washington, coming to a stop with what looked like inches to spare between the airplane and a low building flying a windsock and the American flag.

Merle let me out ahead of him and I staggered down the center aisle and the metal staircase to the ground. I was mighty glad when my feet touched earth. My nerves began to calm. Miss Osborne came up behind me.

'Wasn't that great?' she asked. 'So easy!'

'Yes, ma'am,' I said, pulling myself together. 'It was swell.'

FOUR

An army private with 'McVey' stitched on his khaki shirt presented himself and saluted. He looked about twelve years old, thanks to the freckles that crowded his face and his blond GI haircut.

'We're not in the military, private,' Miss Osborne said, extending her hand. 'No need to salute.'

Flustered, McVey took her hand and pumped it before standing at ease. I wondered if he'd just completed boot camp.

'Ma'am,' he said, 'I'm to take you to the WAC barracks, you'll be bunking there. And you,' he said, looking at Merle, 'you'll be in an enlisted men's barracks nearby.'

'I guess we'll have plenty of roommates, then,' Merle said.

McVey suppressed a grin. 'Not exactly, sir,' he answered. 'After you've had a chance to settle into your quarters I'll take you to meet the base commander and the camp commander. Where are your bags?'

We directed McVey to the baggage compartment under the airplane. He refused Merle's offer of help, carrying all three of our bags to the jeep and stowing them in back. Miss Osborne insisted on carrying the tape recorder herself.

McVey pulled up to a four-story brick barracks, the first in a street full of similar buildings.

'Go on in there,' he said to Merle, pointing toward the door to the barracks, the first of four on a tree-lined street. 'Just pick any bed. I'll be back here in half an hour to take you to the base commander.'

'Sure,' Merle said, retrieving his suitcase and heading for the stairs to the barracks. 'See you all later,' he said.

McVey drove to the end of the street and pulled up to a single-story clapboard house, painted white with bare wooden steps.

'You're quartered here,' he said to Miss Osborne and me.

He jumped out and went around to the back of our jeep to retrieve our bags.

'We can carry our own bags, private,' Miss Osborne said. 'We're not crippled.'

'Ma'am,' McVey said, 'if I let you tote your own luggage my sergeant would have me peeling potatoes for a week.'

We followed him up the steps and into a room with six narrow beds, none of which seemed to be occupied. Sheets, blankets, towels and a pillow lay at the foot of two of the beds.

'Are we the only girls here?' I asked. 'I thought we were bunking with some WACs.'

'Not exactly,' McVey answered. 'Until the prisoners of war arrived three WACs and two army nurses were quartered here.'

'Where are they now?' Miss Osborne asked. 'I hope they didn't have to leave because of us.'

'No, ma'am,' the young private said. 'It was because of the Geneva Convention.'

'I don't understand,' I said to McVey.

'I do,' Miss Osborne said. 'The Geneva Convention says that prisoners of war must live under the same conditions as their captor country's soldiers.'

'Yes, ma'am,' McVey said. 'So all of us assigned to the prisoner-of-war camp have to live in tents as long as the POWs do. When the camp's permanent barracks are built we'll be able to move back into our regular quarters. Before winter, we hope.'

I remembered seeing the orderly rows of white tents north of the base as my airplane was landing. They weren't all behind barbed wire.

'Not the entire base!' I said.

'No, ma'am,' McVey said. 'Just those of us who are assigned to the POW camp. The WACs who bunked here work in the camp administrative office and the nurses are assigned to the camp infirmary.' He drew himself to attention and saluted, then realized he didn't need to, letting his hand fall to his side.

'I'll be back to pick you up in half an hour,' he said.

'Thank you, private,' Miss Osborne said. McVey turned on his heel and left.

In the bathroom of our quarters I filled a glass with water and took my aspirin. I realized we hadn't had lunch and wondered if we would be offered any food before dinner. McVey hadn't mentioned it, and it didn't seem to be on the schedule.

The bathroom wasn't luxurious, but it was roomy, with two sinks, a toilet and a shower. I washed my face and hands and applied powder and lipstick, the only makeup I ever wore. Ada urged me to use mascara and foundation, saying they would make me look younger, but I didn't see the point. I was a thirty-year-old widow and didn't see why I should pretend not to be.

Miss Osborne, Merle, Private McVey and I cooled our heels for two hours waiting to meet the base commander, sitting on a hard wooden bench in the reception area of the base admin-istration building. We watched while dozens of soldiers of various ranks milled about, dispersing down hallways then reappearing again. Then a group coalesced around a tall, balding lieutenant colonel on his way out the door. We stood up and McVey saluted.

'Colonel Peterson, sir,' McVey said.

Peterson paused, his entourage of junior officers collecting around him.

'What, soldier?' Peterson answered him. 'Can't you see I'm leaving the building? I've cancelled the rest of my appoint-ments for today.' His gaze swept over us. 'Who are these civilians and why are they here?'

Miss Osborne spoke up. 'We're from the Morale Operations branch, Office of Strategic Services, here to interview your German prisoners of war.'

Peterson paused. 'Yes,' he said, 'right. Well, welcome to Fort Meade. Do you have everything you need?'

'Yes, thank you,' Miss Osborne said.

'Very good,' he said. 'Perhaps you can join me for dinner one night.'

McVey saluted again, the group of officers left the building and we were left standing there, watching them go.

'I can't believe it,' Merle said. 'He had no idea who we are!'

'That's a good thing,' Miss Osborne said. 'The less he's aware of us and our mission, the better. I don't want any interference from the military.'

I was hungrier than ever.

'What's next?' I said. 'I'm starving.'

'I'm supposed to take you to the prisoner-of-war camp and introduce you to the commander there,' McVey said. 'But we can stop at the PX first, if you want a snack.'

'Please,' Merle said. 'I'm hungry too.'

After waiting in a queue of jostling GIs, I edged myself to the front counter of the mobile PX parked outside the base rec building. I'd never seen so much packed into such a small space in my life. And it wasn't all cigarettes and candy, either.

The GIs could buy everything from toiletries to shoelaces there. I was sure condoms were available under the counter. Even beer was for sale after evening mess.

I found myself averting my eyes from the barbershop magazines. The army felt that access to pictures of practically naked pin-up girls was important to soldiers' morale. We girls had to be happy with movie magazines with Dana Andrews wearing a tux on the cover.

Since I didn't have any idea where my next meal was coming from, I bought a Snickers bar, a bag of Lay's potato chips and a Coke, all the PX soldier behind the counter would let me have. He told me I was entitled to a package of Twinkies too, but I wasn't that desperate. Merle bought a candy bar, cigarettes and a Coke. We rejoined Private McVey and Miss Osborne, who had been waiting for us in the jeep.

'Aren't you hungry?' I said to Miss Osborne as she extended an arm to help me into the back seat. Once seated I tore into my candy bar.

'I had some crackers in my purse,' she said. 'I should have told you to bring snacks. If you miss chow on an army base you're SOL until the mess horn blares.'

McVey backed the jeep around and headed north on the base main road.

'Could it be possible that we are actually going to the

prisoner-of-war camp?' Merle asked him. 'We've been on this damn base for hours.'

'Yes, sir, that's where we're headed,' McVey answered.

'I don't believe it,' Merle said, alternating bites of his candy bar with swigs of Coke.

'Calm down,' Miss Osborne said. 'This is the military. All the necessary rituals and niceties have to be performed before we'll be free to do our job. That's just the way it is.'

Merle mumbled under his breath. 'Where I come from we don't have to wait hours to meet people who don't even remember who we are before we start work.'

If Miss Osborne heard him she didn't respond.

Private McVey drove past a watchtower and a block of white tents and then turned right immediately before reaching a tall, rectangular stockade constructed from two barbed wire fences which ran parallel to each other. The fences were topped with nasty-looking razor wire wrapped in a circle.

McVey parked at a low building with the American flag flying overhead. Another watchtower stood guard over the building. As I climbed out of the jeep I noticed a glint where the sun struck a guard's rifle sight.

'This is the administration building for the prisoner-of-war camp,' McVey said, opening the passenger side door for Miss Osborne. Merle and I clambered out of the back seat yet again. 'You'll meet the commander, Major John Lucas, now.'

'Before midnight?' Merle asked.

'Stop it,' I said, nudging him. 'He's a private, don't pick on him, he can't talk back.'

Inside the building we sat on yet another wooden bench. It wasn't as busy there as the base commander's HQ, but the door labeled 'Camp Commander' remained closed. An hour passed. Finally the door opened and a young army lieutenant emerged.

'Miss Osborne,' he said, reaching out his hand to shake hers. 'It's good to meet you. I'm Lieutenant Gary Rawlins, Major Lucas's Executive Officer.'

'At least this one is expecting us,' Merle muttered.

'Come in, please,' Lt Rawlins said.

The camp commander's office was empty.

'I don't believe it,' Merle said. Miss Osborne shot him a look that silenced him.

'Major Lucas will be available soon,' Lt Rawlins said. 'I'll go tell him you're here.'

Merle waited until Rawlins closed the door behind him. 'At least these chairs are more comfortable than those benches,' he said. 'I wish I'd brought a deck of cards. Or a book.'

After half an hour, which we passed without any conversation, the office door opened and an army major entered, followed by Lt Rawlins. The major's appearance surprised me. He was short, bald and chubby. And at least sixty, I guessed. Not a photogenic candidate for an army recruiting poster. I'd read in the newspaper that most of the POW camp commanders were World War I officers recruited out of retirement, and I could believe this man hadn't worn a military uniform in years.

'Good afternoon, Miss Osborne,' Major Lucas said, in a voice that was more authoritative than his looks. Booming, actually. They shook hands and Miss Osborne introduced us to him.

'Mrs Pearlie is my assistant. Mr Ellison will be working as our translator.'

The major looked at Merle – not with approval, I thought. 'How come you speak German?' he asked. 'You don't look much like a refugee.'

'I'm an American,' Merle said. 'And I'd never been out of Texas before the war started.'

'I don't trust Germans,' the major said. 'I was in the First World War too. I was captured and spent a year in a POW camp in Erfurt. They gave us stewed acorns to eat.'

'I speak German because I learned it from my grandparents, who were immigrants,' Merle said, his face flushing. 'They arrived here in 1889. I'm an American.'

Miss Osborne placed a warning hand on Merle's arm.

The major shrugged. 'All right then, let's get down to business,' he said, sitting down behind his desk.

We pulled our chairs over to his desk. Lt Rawlins stood behind Lucas, leaning against a file cabinet.

'Please take notes, Mrs Pearlie,' Miss Osborne said.

I pulled out my steno pad and a pencil. I hadn't had a chance to review my shorthand manual yet, but I figured I could muddle through.

'We're here to interview your German prisoners of war,' Miss Osborne said to Major Lucas. 'Our mission is to identify those who might be able to assist us and recruit them for an OSS operation.'

'As double agents?' Lucas asked.

'Not exactly,' Miss Osborne said. 'We need them to deliver black propaganda materials behind German lines in Italy and perhaps inside Germany itself.'

'You can't trust a one of them. Whoever you send behind German lines will betray you.'

'We don't think so,' Miss Osborne said. 'Our research tells us that ordinary German soldiers can be successfully recruited. Especially if we ask them to do tasks that don't directly result in German deaths.'

'They're all Nazis, whether they are party members or not. I spent a hellish year in their company in 1917. I understand the German personality very well.'

'The OSS has done advanced psychological studies in this area,' Miss Osborne said. 'We're convinced we can recruit suitable men who will be eager to shorten the war and spare their families and friends.'

'Whatever you say; it's your mission,' Lucas said. 'You'll just have to figure it out for yourself. I'll do what I can to assist you, of course. I'm eating dinner tonight in the German POW mess hall. Would you like to join me? You can get a first look at your subjects.'

'Yes, absolutely,' Miss Osborne said.

'Good,' he said. 'Do you have a driver?'

'Yes.'

'Have him drop you off before the main gate to the stockade just before six. Lt Rawlins will meet you and escort you to the mess hall. Oh, Lieutenant, give Miss Osborne a list of the German internees.'

'One more question,' Miss Osborne said.

'Yes?'

'I understand that two of the German prisoners died at sea?'

'Yes. They simply vanished, and there's only one way to disappear at sea. Overboard. The ship's captain and security officer investigated and concluded the men had committed suicide.'

Lt Rawlins escorted us outside.

'Let me orient you to the camp while it's still daylight,' he said. 'We don't have to go inside the stockade; it would be easier to see it from the watchtower.'

We clambered up a long ladder and into the square confines of the watchtower. Two MPs saluted but Rawlins put them at ease and they returned to their stations, keeping watch over the camp with rifles ready.

'Those tents you saw when you drove in, the ones that are outside the stockade fence, that's where camp personnel are living until the prisoners' barracks are completed. We have an officers' mess and club, a hospital, a PX and a laundry. Everything you'd find in a regular military camp.'

We turned around to view the prisoner-of-war camp itself. I guessed it was about fifteen hundred feet from where we stood to the other end of the camp, which I could see was bordered by a road. It wasn't quite as wide. Three double rows of tents filled the compound.

'Most of the camp is occupied by the Italian prisoners of war. As you're looking at the camp, the lower section of tents, on the left, are the Germans. We strung another stockade fence between them.'

'Why did you separate the Germans and the Italians?' Miss Osborne asked.

'The dagos hate the Krauts' very guts,' Rawlins said. 'Have you heard what the German military is doing in Italy? The Italian people are starving. The Germans have requisitioned all eggs, meat, milk, vegetables and fruit. German troops are firing at hungry crowds storming food shops. They're looting the occupied regions, not just of food, but also of gold, silver and art. The Roman Catholic church has closed all its churches except St Peter's because of plundering.'

'No wonder the Italians hate them,' I said.

'We've set the camp up so the Germans have separate mess tents, PXs, infirmaries and football fields. The Italians stand at the fence and scream insults at the Germans all day long. If they were housed together we'd be breaking up fights between them constantly.'

FIVE

Once back in our quarters Miss Osborne sat down on her bed and pulled off her shoes.

'My God,' she said, 'what a day. I'm glad we flew instead of drove, aren't you? Otherwise we would still be out there meeting people.'

'Yes, ma'am,' I said. And then, just for my own planning purposes, I asked, 'Do you fly often?'

'As much as I can,' she answered, unbuttoning the waistband of her skirt and heaving a sigh of relief. 'What did you think of flying?'

If I wanted to be successful at this job I knew what my answer had to be. 'I thought it was grand.'

'After a while you'll think of it no differently than a jeep ride,' she said.

I doubted that.

I followed Miss Osborne's example and took off my own shoes and loosened my clothing while Miss Osborne rummaged in her suitcase. She pulled out a flask.

'Bourbon?' she asked, holding the flask toward me.

'Yes, ma'am, thank you!' I answered.

'I'm glad you're not one of those teetotalers,' she said, pouring hefty shots into two GI-issued metal cups she produced from her suitcase. 'I hate to drink alone.'

'Thank you,' I said, sipping mine gratefully. It wasn't a martini, but it would do.

'Tell me,' she said, 'what did you think of today?'

'What do you mean?' I asked. I wasn't accustomed to being asked my opinion by my boss.

Miss Osborne propped her pillow against the wall and leaned back, stretching her legs out on the bed.

'I'd like to know your impressions, Louise, that's all,' she said.

I collected myself. I intended to keep this job, so I wanted whatever I said to be well considered. And diplomatic.

'Start with Merle,' she said.

That took me by surprise. I liked Merle, but that wasn't what Miss Osborne was looking for.

'He's impatient,' I said. 'And says too much in public. He's too impolitic to work in the field.'

'I agree,' she said. 'I'll talk to him, but if he doesn't improve he'll have to be satisfied with forgery. Why do you think I chose him for this mission? Other than the shortage of translators.'

I didn't have a clue. Best admit it instead of waffling.

'I don't know,' I said.

Miss Osborne nodded and swallowed a slug of bourbon. 'Good,' she said. 'I like an honest person. I chose Merle because he is so colorful. I mean, that accent! Those boots! Wonderful distractions for anyone he's interviewing.'

'Like us,' I said. 'No one expects serious business from women.'

We finished our bourbon. That and the aspirin I took after we arrived soothed my aching back and headache.

'Back to your impressions,' Miss Osborne said. 'What about the camp commander, Major Lucas, what did you think of him?'

'He wasn't what you would call combat ready,' I said. 'I think he probably came out of retirement to do this job. And he had a bad opinion of all Germans, whether they are Nazis or not. Even Americans of German descent.'

'Agreed,' she said. 'I don't think we'll see much of him. I expect his XO runs the camp. What's your impression of Rawlins?'

'He seems competent,' I said. 'But he's young and fit; I wonder why he was assigned this duty. A prisoner-of-war camp in the States is a backwater station for a young military officer.'

A knock sounded at the door.

'Are you decent? Can I come in?' Merle called out.

'Sure,' Miss Osborne answered him.

Merle entered our room. 'Do you two know that I am the

only human being quartered in a four-story barracks? It's loony.' He sniffed. 'You're drinking bourbon!'

'Want some?' Miss Osborne asked. 'Did you bring a cup?'

'No,' Merle said.

'I'll rinse mine out,' I said. Going into the bathroom I ran water over my cup. I didn't want another drink myself. Having Miss Osborne as my boss was going to require all the mental alertness I could muster.

Miss Osborne poured herself another stiff drink and filled Merle's up until he said, 'Enough!'

She looked at me. 'You don't want another?'

'No, thank you,' I said. 'One is enough.'

'Wise woman,' she said. 'I inherited my tolerance to bourbon from my father, fortunately for me.'

Merle loosened his tie and undid the top button of his shirt.

'Interesting day. I was surprised at what Lucas said, that those German POWs killed themselves on the way to the States,' he said. 'It doesn't make sense. You'd think they'd be elated to leave the front.'

'We don't know they killed themselves,' Miss Osborne said.

'But Lucas said they did,' Merle said.

Miss Osborne turned to me. 'Louise, what do you think?'

'I suspect the authorities just assumed that they committed suicide,' I answered. 'I haven't heard any real evidence that they did. Just that they vanished, and overboard was the only place they could go. And they were German prisoners of war. I doubt the ship's captain cared enough to investigate.'

'What else could have happened to them?' Merle said.

'They could have fallen,' I answered. 'Those POWs were packed like sardines on the transport ship. They were allowed two hours a day outside in shifts. I saw a picture of it in *Life*. They filled the entire deck, from bow to stern. I mean, they could have been sitting on the rail and fallen overboard when the ocean surged.'

'Or they were helped overboard,' Miss Osborne said. 'By one of their fellow prisoners.'

'You mean murdered!' I said, shocked. 'Why?'

Miss Osborne shrugged. 'I don't know,' she said. 'But if

there's a murderer in our POW camp I'd like to know who he is.'

Private McVey stopped the jeep at the stockade gate. The guard in the watchtower overhead leaned over the rail to scrutinize us, his rifle at the ready. An MP stationed at the gate greeted us and took the papers McVey handed him, examined them, then handed them back. 'Welcome to the Fritz Ritz,' he said, waving us inside the stockade. The gate closed behind us with a metallic clang. We were inside a prisoner-of-war camp, along with over sixteen hundred Axis soldiers and their jailers. I felt a surge of excitement and anticipation. I'd recovered from the airplane flight and was thrilled to be away from the Registry and its jungle of file cabinets. This was an adventure!

We climbed out of the jeep in front of the German mess tent. Inside three men waited for us at a head table guarded by two more MPs. Major Lucas and Lt Rawlins and a third person, hidden by Rawlins' body, were drinking from cut crystal sherry glasses that looked tiny in their hands. Colored mess attendants in spotless white uniforms were loading up three cafeteria stations with steaming containers of food. It smelled wonderful! I hadn't had a meal since breakfast and I was ravenous.

Lucas offered the three of us sherry, but taking Miss Osborne's lead, Merle and I declined.

'If you say so,' Lucas said, refilling his own glass. 'I cannot watch these men eat the same rations as an American soldier without fortification.'

Rawlins moved aside, revealing the third man in the group. I would have known him anywhere. He was in his late thirties, fit and dressed conservatively in a blue suit and dark tie, like all G-men. His fedora sported a small yellow feather stuck in the hatband.

'Mrs Pearlie, it's good to see you again. You must think I'm shadowing you,' the man said.

'I don't think it, I know it,' I said, shaking his hand.

'You've met, obviously,' Rawlins said to me. He turned to

Miss Osborne and Merle. 'This is Agent Gray Williams, our FBI liaison.' I knew there was an FBI agent assigned to every prisoner-of-war camp, but I never expected that the agent attached to Fort Meade would be a man I knew and would rather never have seen again.

'Let's get our food,' Lucas said. 'The prisoners will be coming in soon.'

The mess boys loaded my plate with thick slices of meatloaf, mashed potatoes, peas, rolls and real butter, until food filled my plate to its edge. I selected a wedge of blueberry pie for dessert. I'd almost forgotten what a meal without the limitations of rationing could look like.

Once we were seated at the head table the prisoners filed in.

Each German prisoner wore a GI khaki shirt and trousers, with 'PW' stenciled on the back of the shirt. Their ranks weren't obvious, but I'd bet my dress shoe ration stamp that the poised, confident prisoner who sat at the head of the table closest to us was a high-ranking officer.

Williams, who had sat down next to me, leaned over and said in a low voice, 'See that one?', nodding at the prisoner I'd noticed.

'I do,' I said.

'He's SS-Sturmbannführer Dieter Kapp, Waffen SS. Major Kapp to you. He commanded an SS flame tank platoon in North Africa. He's the ranking prisoner here and the POW's spokesman, their commanding officer really, and a hardcore Nazi. The prisoners don't use the latrine unless he says it's OK.'

'Waffen SS!' I said. I looked at Kapp more closely. He was thin and wiry with deep-set blue eyes and narrow lips, sitting almost at attention in his chair. The men on either side of him looked uncomfortable being there. Yes, I could picture Major Kapp strutting around in a coal black uniform with 'SS' tabs on the collar and a skull and crossbones patch on the cap.

'Kapp is the only prisoner who speaks English,' Williams said. 'And none of the guards speak German. We have a German translator assigned to the base, but he's spread thin.

So Kapp is our only conduit to the prisoners most of the time.'

'Over there,' he continued, nodding toward the group again, 'the one with light brown hair and a scar, Lt Bahnsen, he was conscripted out of a Lutheran seminary. He was a navigator for the Luftwaffe. His reconnaissance plane was shot down and he was the only survivor.'

That crash must have been the cause of the livid red scar that began on the man's temple and coursed down his left cheek. Whatever had caused it had barely missed his left eye.

'And the small dark stocky one on our Lutheran's right, the one with big hands, he's just a private. Hans Marek is his name. But he's an ethnic Pole, he can't love the Nazis.'

Williams squinted, searching the Germans for another face. 'I don't see Jens Geller,' he said. 'Perhaps he's ill. He's another fellow I wanted to point out to you. Whenever the German translator comes by the camp Geller peppers him with questions about the war. Apparently he has brothers still in the Wehrmacht. He might be someone interested in the war ending sooner rather than later. Anyway, those three men would be good candidates for your team to interview.'

I shot my eyes at him. 'You know our mission?'

'Of course. I'm the FBI's ears and eyes here.'

'Just what does that mean?'

'Mrs Pearlie, you know what information interests Director Hoover.'

Yes, I did. Director Hoover was interested in any scrap of gossip, dirt or intelligence he could collect on almost anyone in the United States. Only children were exempt from his curiosity, and I wasn't sure about that.

Cynicism aside, the FBI was in charge of counterintelligence inside the United States. Williams would want to know if any of the prisoners had family or contacts in the country, training in sabotage or an inclination to escape and create havoc.

'I can count on you to relay any information you learn in your interviews that I should know,' Williams said, 'can't I?'

'Of course,' I said. I wasn't about to share anything with

Williams unless Miss Osborne instructed me to, but I saw no reason to tell him so.

'You'll start the process tomorrow?'

'Yes,' I said. 'The sooner we begin, when the prisoners are still disoriented from the trip, the more likely we can penetrate their defenses.'

'You're only interested in the Germans, am I right?' Lt Rawlins asked.

'Yes,' I said. I scanned the alphabetized list he'd given me. No Rein Hermann, thank goodness. 'The Italians will be interrogated by another team.'

'They'll be easier nuts to crack,' Rawlins said.

After dinner Lt Rawlins had asked me to come back to his desk in the administration building to pick up the prisoner information he had set aside for me, leaving the rest of our dinner party to chat over coffee in the officer's lounge.

'Does this include the names of the two Germans who died during the crossing?' I asked.

'Yes, here they are, the ones marked with crosses.'

Rolf Muntz, twenty-five, and Hurst Aach, twenty-three. I wondered why men so young, escaping the battlefield to ride out the rest of the war many miles away from it, would want to kill themselves.

'Do you want their paybooks?' Rawlins asked.

'Yes, please.'

'I'll need them back as soon as possible.' Rawlins handed me a stack of booklets about the size of passports. Every German soldier had one of these paybooks, called a *Soldbuch*, which contained much more information than pay records. Up to seventeen pages long, the booklets contained all a German soldier's records, including pay, awards, stations and home addresses. Merle would have quite a job translating them all.

'Thanks,' I said, stuffing the papers and booklets into my bag. I stuck my hand out to shake his. 'You've been a great help.'

Lt Rawlins held my hand a bit longer than necessary. I wasn't really surprised. On a military base women were in short supply, and even a thirty-year-old widow such as myself could expect plenty of attention from men, none of it serious.

'Are you going to be on base this weekend?' Rawlins asked.

'I don't know,' I answered.

'I'm off duty on Saturday,' he said. 'We could go to a movie.'

'I don't think so,' I said, edging toward the door. 'It depends. If I'm here I'm sure I'll be working.'

Rawlins looked disappointed, and I felt bad that I'd been so dismissive. But I just wasn't interested. Knowing Joe was back in DC occupied any romantic ideas I had.

'Do you mind if I smoke?' Merle asked.

'Not at all,' Miss Osborne said. Merle lit one of his PX cigarettes and watched as Miss Osborne and I spread out all the pay booklets Lt Rawlins had given me on one of the empty beds in our billet.

'Do we have the paybooks for the Germans that went overboard?' she asked me.

'Rolf Muntz and Hurst Aach,' I said. 'Yes, we do.' I grabbed up their booklets and opened them. I couldn't read most of the German, of course, but I could decipher the names of towns. 'That's interesting, they're both from the same place. Reichenberg.'

'That's in Czechoslovakia,' Merle said. 'Or was. The Sudetenland.' Which had been annexed by Germany in 1938 on the pretext that most of its citizens were German-speaking.

'Interesting,' Miss Osborne said. 'I wonder if they were conscripts.'

Merle took the two paybooks and skimmed them quickly.

'These guys lived at the same address,' he said. 'Maybe a boarding house.'

'Odd,' Miss Osborne said. 'How likely is it that they would both find themselves on the same Liberty Ship headed for the States, and then kill themselves? On the same damn day?'

Realizing that these two men might have known each other made me even more suspicious about their deaths.

'Let's not forget them.' I was glad to hear Miss Osborne say that. 'Louise, find Major Dieter Kapp's paybook. He'll be the first person we interview.'

'You think he might cooperate with us?' Merle asked.

'Not at all. The man is SS. But I still need to talk with him. He's the commanding officer of the Germans in the camp and I want to get a feel for how doctrinaire he is. Besides, it's good psychology to address the officers first.'

'Agent Williams suggested three men who are likely candidates for us to turn,' I said. 'One is a lieutenant who was conscripted out of a Lutheran seminary. The second is an ethnic Pole, and the third has family in the Wehrmacht.'

Merle shuffled the paybooks. 'Here's the priest,' he said, 'Alfred Bahnsen. He was halfway through his final year when he was drafted. And the Pole's name is Hans Marek. Marek is a Polish surname.'

'OK,' Miss Osborne said. 'Tomorrow our first interview will be with our SS tank commander, Major Kapp. Then we'll follow with Bahnsen and Marek. Merle, please look through all the paybooks tonight and let me know anything you find that's unusual.'

Miss Osborne glanced at the door. Merle understood that he had been dismissed. He gathered up the paperwork he needed and left for his lonely barracks.

'Louise,' Miss Osborne said, 'tell me about Gray Williams.'

I knew this was coming. Miss Osborne was bound to ask me how I happened to be acquainted with the FBI agent who was assigned to the Fort Meade POW camp.

'I met Gray Williams the first time when someone – someone I knew, although I never found out her name – called the FBI and complained that I was drinking with a Frenchman in a hotel bar. Which I was. I'd met him at a party. He worked at the French embassy. Agent Williams called on me at home and warned me that government girls with Top Secret security clearance shouldn't date foreigners.'

'Oh, for God's sake,' Miss Osborne said. 'I've never approved of the FBI vetting OSS employees and keeping files on them. How would he know you weren't on an assignment?'

I left out the part about how my friendship with the Frenchman at the hotel bar was part of an unauthorized honey trap I'd set to get into the Vichy French embassy to steal files. Miss Osborne didn't need to know that. This was the start of my continuing worry that the FBI would find out I was seeing Joe, Czech accent and all.

'The second time I met Agent Williams I actually worked with him,' I continued. 'I was OSS liaison to a group, including the FBI, who were investigating an incident on the Western Shore of Maryland. It began with a suspicious postcard that the US Censor's Office had sent the OSS.'

'I remember that,' she said. 'I read about it in your file. That was quite an adventure.'

'Yes, ma'am, it was,' I said.

'Is there anything else you need to tell me about Williams?'

'Not that I should,' I said.

Miss Osborne thought about my response, staring at me with one eyebrow raised. 'All right,' she said. 'I asked for an assistant who could keep secrets, and it looks like I got one.'

'Thank you,' I said. So far in my career I'd never regretted keeping my mouth shut. Besides, no one could stop me from thinking whatever I liked.

'You'll let me know if Agent Williams tells you anything I should know.'

'Of course,' I said.

The next morning we were escorted to the tent we were to use for interviews. It was fairly close to the stockade gate, under the main watchtower, and held two tables pushed together and several chairs. Miss Osborne set up our tape recorder, plugging it into an electric outlet mounted on a pole outside the tent. We'd be guarded by an MP standing watch outside and another inside, who'd also escort the prisoner to and from his quarters.

'Louise,' Miss Osborne said. 'I want you to take notes on our conversations. Not about the substance of them – they're being recorded and a typist will transcribe them later. I want to know your impressions and thoughts about the prisoners and their suitability for our work. Merle, I know Major Kapp speaks English, but please stay. I'd like you to hear what he has to say.'

SIX

Major Dieter Kapp would have been the perfect model SS officer for an Allied propaganda poster. He was thin but muscular, with clear Aryan blue eyes and blond hair cut short. He sat in the cheap wooden chair with an arrogant posture and attitude that didn't correspond with his current situation, crossing his legs casually and taking his time lighting an unfiltered cigarette by striking a match across the edge of the table. Even the demeaning luggage tag still secured to one of his shirt buttons didn't diminish his self-possession. He exhaled his cigarette smoke as if he was an actor in a film noir, and regarded us the way a bachelor uncle might tolerate a crowd of noisy children. I could easily picture him ordering a platoon of flame tanks to incinerate whatever stood in his way.

'Who are you? Why are there no officers here to interrogate me?' he asked us, in English with a British accent. 'I am the senior German officer in this camp.'

Miss Osborne didn't answer his question.

'Major Kapp,' she said, checking the short handwritten paragraph of information Merle had gleaned from Kapp's paybook. 'You commanded a platoon of flame tanks in North Africa? And your platoon was part of the Twenty-first Panzer Division?'

'You already know this,' he said. 'You are wasting my time.'

'You have somewhere else to be?' Miss Osborne said. 'The crafts tent, perhaps?'

Kapp took a long pull from his cigarette and stared at her with condescension. Miss Osborne didn't flinch.

'Prior to your assignment to the Twenty-first Panzer Division you were stationed in Poland and then in the Sudetenland, is that correct?' she continued. 'Then transferred to North Africa?'

'Correct,' he said.

'And you were captured at Tunis?'

'I was.'

'You surrendered your entire command also, I see. Without exchanging any gunfire with Allied troops.'

Kapp's eyes narrowed. 'We were overwhelmed. It would have been useless to resist.'

Miss Osborne ignored his response and continued. 'You are a member of the Nazi Party?'

'Of course,' he said. 'I am SS, Waffen Schutzstaffel. You know that. You continue to waste my time.'

'Your next of kin is your mother, who is living in Switzerland? Why does your mother live in Switzerland? Isn't she German?'

Kapp stubbed out his cigarette and uncrossed his legs, leaning across the table toward us. 'Certainly she is German. She moved to Switzerland after my father died to live with her sister.'

'Major Kapp, do your surrender and your mother's residence have anything to do with how you view the progress of the war? Do you think that Germany is losing?'

'No,' he said, his voice clipped. 'I am confident of a German victory. And I am committed to the Nazi Party and to the Führer. God is on the side of the Reich, our victory is destined. Every German soldier in this camp believes this. You will not get any intelligence or cooperation from any of them, I guarantee you.' He half rose from his seat as if to leave, until the MP guarding him shoved him back into his chair. He didn't like that, and he showed it by leaning over the table and crushing his cigarette into shreds, not in the ashtray at his seat, but in the one between Merle and Miss Osborne, all the while staring directly at her.

Miss Osborne didn't flinch. I scribbled my brief impression of Kapp in my steno book. 'A dangerous, evil man.' The tape recorder turned, recording pure silence, while Kapp and Miss Osborne conducted their staring contest. Kapp's eyes were the first to blink, so he leaned back in his chair, ostensibly to light another cigarette.

'Major Kapp, what do you know about the two men who killed themselves on the trip across the Atlantic? Their names were Hurst Aach and Rolf Muntz.'

'They were German foot soldiers, *Schützen*, that is all I know. And cowards and traitors for killing themselves.'

'You didn't know them personally?'

'Certainly not. Didn't I say they were just foot soldiers? I commanded a tank platoon.'

'We both know,' Miss Osborne said, changing the subject, 'that you possess information that would interest our military. The sooner the war ends the sooner you could join your mother in Switzerland. Until then we could arrange preferential treatment.'

'I would rather never see my mother again than betray Germany,' Kapp said.

I believed him and added that impression to my notes.

After an MP escorted Kapp out of the interview room, Miss Osborne exhaled in relief and I flexed my right hand, cramped from gripping my pencil tightly.

'Well,' she said. 'No surprises there. As long as Kapp is the senior German officer I'm afraid we will have a difficult time recruiting volunteers for our operation.'

'How can he stop them?' I asked.

'You'll see,' she said.

Leutnant Alfred Bahnsen had a black eye, a bad one. His right eye was almost closed. Added to the long, livid scar on his face it gave him a damaged look.

'Lt Bahnsen, your eye looks very painful,' Miss Osborne said. 'Have you had it attended to?'

'Yes, ma'am,' he said, in rapid German. 'I've seen the medical officer. He gave me some aspirin. And I need to keep this ice bag on it.' He held up the bag and pressed it to his injured eye, wincing as the ice cold met his face.

'What happened?' she asked.

'I fell,' he said. 'Hit the edge of my bunk.'

The army MP, a husky man with 'Steesen' stamped on his pocket who stood guard at the tent door, rolled his eyes. 'Bahnsen is lying about his black eye,' I wrote in my notes. 'Ask Steesen about it later.'

'That's a shame,' Miss Osborne said. She pushed the 'on'

switch on the tape recorder and our second interview began. Bahnsen kept the ice bag pressed to his injured eye.

'You are a lieutenant in the Luftwaffe, I believe. Your plane was shot down at El Alamein.'

'Yes,' he said, in English. 'And you can tell your translator to take a coffee break. I speak English.'

'What?' Miss Osborne said. 'Why didn't we know that?'

'I don't want Major Kapp to know. I don't trust him, and this way I can monitor what he says to you Americans. I'd appreciate it if you keep this a secret.'

'It won't leave here,' Miss Osborne said, looking pointedly at the MP, who nodded. 'You were attending a Lutheran seminary before the war, weren't you?' she continued.

'I was. I was conscripted in my final year.'

'Odd for a priest to go to war,' she said.

'I'm not ordained. I was the flight navigator for a photographic reconnaissance plane. I couldn't defy conscription, I have family in Berlin. God understands. He doesn't require perfection of any of us, even a priest.'

'Are you a member of the Reich Church, or of the Confessing Church?'

Bahnsen started. His expression changed from resignation to wariness, and his one good eye flickered away from us.

'What do you mean?' he said.

Miss Osborne made a show of shuffling her papers. 'If you are a Lutheran you must be either a member of the Nazi wing of the Lutheran church, or with Dietrich Bonhoeffer's group, the Confessing Church.'

'I've never met Bonhoeffer. He was banned from teaching in Berlin before I even arrived there.'

'If you were a Lutheran student of theology surely you would have discussed Bonheoffer often with your fellow students.'

'I'm not political. I'm not a Nazi; regular soldiers of the Luftwaffe are not permitted to belong to a political party.'

'You must know that Bonhoeffer now resides in Tegel Prison.'

'I did near that.'

'Do you think the Nazis will execute him?' Miss Osborne asked. 'What a shame that would be, such a brilliant theologian.'

Tears began to dribble from Bahnsen's eyes. He put down the ice bag and sopped up the moisture from his face with a handkerchief that he pulled out of his pants pocket.

'My eye is extremely painful,' he said. 'I would like to go now, please.'

'Is he crying because of his injuries, or because of Bonhoeffer?' I wrote in my notes.

'One more question and then you can leave,' Miss Osborne said. 'Did you know Hurst Aach and Rolf Muntz?'

'The men who disappeared on our way across the ocean? Vaguely. We were kept in the same hold. The two of them knew each other before the war and spent most of their time together.'

'You said disappeared,' Miss Osborne said. 'You don't believe they committed suicide?'

'I don't know,' Bahnsen said. 'I don't know anything about what happened.'

Miss Osborne nodded at Steesen, the MP who escorted Bahnsen out of the interview room.

Miss Osborne turned off the tape recorder so we could talk freely.

'I know who Dietrich Bonhoeffer is,' I said. 'But what is the Reich Church?

'The wing of the Lutheran church that's allied with Hitler,' she said. 'Hard to imagine, isn't it? What did you think of Bahnsen? Do you think we can use him?'

'I don't know yet. He seemed a bit timid to me, but the mission won't be that dangerous for a native German speaker, will it?'

'No, but it will require conviction. His religious bent might help us; if he was a member of the Reich Church I think he would have said so, not pretended he'd never heard of it. Perhaps he is anti-Nazi. Let's give our almost-priest some time to think things over before we approach him again. When he's not in pain. I find it hard to believe he got that shiner in a fall.'

'Did you see the MP's expression when Bahnsen said that? He rolled his eyes. As if he knew that story isn't true,' Merle said.

'I'll find out what he knows about it,' I said.

'You do that, Louise. You're less formidable than I am.' Miss Osborne glanced at her watch. 'Thank God,' she said, 'lunchtime. I'm ravenous.'

I found Steesen on his way to the enlisted men's mess. 'Corporal Steesen,' I said to him.

'Ma'am?' he said.

'I need to ask you a question.'

'Yes, ma'am.'

'When we were interviewing Lt Bahnsen and he told us how he'd been injured, you rolled your eyes, as if you knew he wasn't telling the truth.'

Steesen removed his white helmet and ran his fingers through his hair before replacing it. 'Yes, ma'am, I'm sorry. My sergeant says I got to learn to control my facial expressions.'

'What happened to Bahnsen?'

'Major Kapp had a couple of his thugs beat him up.'

'Why?'

'I don't know. They were screaming at him, but I can't speak German, ma'am, none of us can. But Major Kapp, he's the senior German officer. He's in charge. The prisoners, they do what he says. Or else. So I reckon he ordered it.'

'You don't intervene if there's trouble?'

'Ma'am, if that SS bastard keeps the camp under control it's a lot less work for us. Seeing how we don't know what's going on anyway.'

'This is the best tuna sandwich I've had in years,' Merle said, as he bit into the soft white bread filled with a layer of tuna and mayonnaise an inch thick.

'The Army School for Bakers and Cooks is on this base. We eat real good most of the time,' McVey said.

Miss Osborne and I were reveling in the lack of rationing too, enjoying hamburgers that weren't stretched with oatmeal.

'Ice cream next,' Merle said.

Miss Osborne wiped her mouth and pushed her plate away. 'First, work,' she said. 'Merle, can you suggest any potential candidates we can interview this afternoon? That is, in addition to Jens Geller and Hans Marek, whom Agent Williams suggested to us?'

'Yes, ma'am,' he said, pulling his notes out of his jacket pocket. 'I would recommend Thomas Hanzi.'

'Is Hanzi a German surname?' I asked.

'It's not common,' he said. 'It's more Hungarian in origin, I think. I'm curious about the man. He's young, just nineteen; he was unemployed at the time he was conscripted. He's a laborer with an engineering squad, which means he digs ditches. Maybe he's someone the Reich good-times parade passed by.'

There were plenty of those, I thought, just about anyone who didn't fit into the Aryan mold.

'It's worth looking into,' Miss Osborne said. She turned to McVey. 'Private, would you please tell Commander Lucas that we'd like to interview Hans Marek and Thomas Hanzi this afternoon. Then come back here and pick us up, please. We'll get to Geller later today.'

After McVey left Miss Osborne relaxed into her seat. 'Let's bolster ourselves with ice cream, cigarettes and coffee before we head back to the salt mines,' she said.

Our interview with Hans Marek was tough going.

'His German is heavily accented,' Merle said. 'I can barely understand him.'

'Take your time,' Miss Osborne said.

Miss Osborne asked Marek questions, Merle translated her sentences slowly and Marek answered even more slowly. It was like herding a cow through quicksand. Little by little a picture of Marek emerged. He was a native Pole, although he had been living in Germany, working as a stevedore in Bremerhaven, when he was drafted. He explained that his family owned a dairy farm in Silesia. A private, Marek loaded and unloaded military supplies at a depot outside Tunis and was taken prisoner when the Allied front rolled over it, hiding under a Mercedes-Benz utility truck until the firefight was over.

'Ask him if he is a Pole or a German first,' Miss Osborne said.

After Merle spoke to him, Marek laughed, but the tone of his voice when he answered was sarcastic. Merle nodded. 'He says there is no Poland, only the Reich, and anyone who doesn't see this is a fool.'

'But if Germany loses the war, then Poland might be free again,' Miss Osborne said. After Merle translated Marek looked at her as if she was insane.

'Such a thing is not possible,' Marek said.

'The Germans have surrendered in North Africa, the Italians have surrendered, why isn't it possible?'

Marek didn't answer, but he looked interested.

'Think about it,' Miss Osborne said. 'And one last question. Did you know Aach and Muntz, the men who died on the Atlantic crossing?'

Marek shrugged, unconcerned. 'Hardly. What fools they were! Here there is plenty to eat and drink and a cot with a mattress. And no one shooting at you. It's like heaven with beer.'

Miss Osborne nodded at the MP to escort Marek from the room, but first the POW pulled out a handful of items from a bulging pocket.

'All for sale,' he said in terrible English, and then turned to Merle to translate the rest of his pitch.

'He wants money for beer from the PX,' Merle said, 'and he has souvenirs to sell.'

Marek laid his merchandise on the table in front of us. A trench cigarette lighter, a silver wound badge (comparable to our Purple Heart), an empty matchbox stamped with the German eagle and a stained ribbon bar.

'For goodness' sakes,' Miss Osborne said. 'Tell him we aren't interested in buying his trash.'

'I wonder how much he wants for the lighter,' Merle said. He spoke in German to Marek, who answered him back. 'He says it works, just needs fluid. Ten bucks.'

Merle dug into his back pocket for his wallet, but Miss Osborne put a restraining hand on his arm. 'Collecting German souvenirs is against regulations. Period.'

Merle, clearly disappointed, shook his head at Marek, who grinned and stuffed his trinkets back into his pocket.

'Someone will buy that lighter,' Merle grumbled. 'Why can't I?'

Schütze Thomas Hanzi was an extraordinarily handsome young man, barely more than a teenager. He had coal-black hair, olive skin, a chiseled face, slim build and, I swear, eyes so blue they were almost violet. He was definitely not Aryan, except for his eyes.

I wasn't the only one who noticed Hanzi's looks. Miss Osborne leaned over and whispered in my ear, 'Roma.' Hanzi was a gypsy; only his blue eyes, thanks to whatever ancestor bestowed them on him, had prevented him from being locked up in a camp somewhere for being too impure even to dig ditches for the Nazi war machine. Just thinking about it made my heart ache for the millions who didn't fit into the Nazi plan for the future of Europe. Miss Osborne caught my expression and I saw worry in her eyes too. She turned off the tape recorder for a minute.

'If we did turn him,' she whispered to Merle and me, 'Private Hanzi wouldn't last an hour behind German lines. If he wasn't attached to a German labor detail he'd be halted, searched and executed immediately. But we should interview him anyway,' she continued. 'We don't want the other prisoners of war to notice anything different about the way we treat him.' She started the tape recorder again.

We needed to keep Hanzi in the interview room as long as the others to protect him from reprisals. Merle just spoke to him conversationally. Hanzi told us he'd been a street sweeper, living in a gypsy ghetto, leaving it only to work and to take a meal of black bread and barley soup at a Nazi Party soup kitchen, until he'd been drafted. He had no idea where the rest of his family was.

Hanzi told us that he and the other prisoners of war were

stunned when they arrived in the United States. They had been told it was a smoking ruin near collapse. Instead the size of the country, the number of automobiles, buses and trains, the amount of food at meals astounded them. They'd been issued clean clothes, towels and blankets. They could shower whenever they wanted. They got two packs of cigarettes a day, free. They could even buy beer at the PX after dinner!

'I don't care if I never return to Germany,' he said.

After a suitable passage of time Miss Osborne had the MP escort Hanzi back to the stockade.

When we'd been left alone in the interview room Miss Osborne turned off the tape recorder again. 'Private Hanzi will be much safer right here in an American prisoner-of-war camp than he would be back in Europe,' she said, shaking her head. 'If it weren't for those eyes he might already be a dead man instead of a ditch digger.'

It was late in the day but we still had time for one more interview. Miss Osborne consulted her notes, then called the MP over. 'We need to see Jens Geller,' she said. 'We requested his presence. Why haven't you brought him in?'

'Ma'am,' Steesen said, 'prisoner Geller has been placed on bread and water, in solitary confinement, for today. I asked Lt Rawlins if he could be released for this interview, but he said no.'

'We'll have to talk to him another time, then,' Miss Osborne said. 'What did Geller do to get punished?'

'Socked a guard, ma'am. The guard called him a German pig. Guess he knows some English.'

'How about Felix Steiner, then?'

When Steiner came into the tent I was astonished to see that the man wore his Panzer beret and carried a walking stick, which looked absurd, to say the least. The only way he could get away with wearing the beret was to rip off the SS insignia, including the skull and crossbones. Without hesitation he introduced himself as Obersturmführer Felix Steiner, an Austrian SS officer, and made sure we understood that his father was a Nazi Party member and a high-ranking official in the Viennese police force. He confirmed that he was the second in command of a signals battalion of the Twenty-first Panzer Division and that he had surrendered at Tunis. He insisted he did not know Major Kapp personally. 'The Twenty-first was the largest tank division in history,' he said, 'and it will be one day again.' He then folded his arms across his chest and refused to answer any more questions. 'Pretentious fool,' I wrote in my notes.

I was pleased to see that Major Lucas, the camp commander, wasn't having dinner in the POW mess with the rest of us tonight. I didn't like the man much and I found his attitude irritating. Lt Rawlins was the senior officer in the group that gathered to have sherry before dinner was served. Even though we hadn't had time for a drink in our barracks before dinner, Miss Osborne refused a sherry. I followed her example and turned away the tiny cut glass that Rawlins offered me. Merle took one though, drained it and requested a refill.

Agent Williams was the last of the American group to enter the mess tent. He was accompanied by a middle-aged, balding man in GI khakis wearing an International Red Cross armband, whom he introduced as Lucien Chantal. He was the camp's liaison with the Red Cross, here to protect the interests of the German prisoners. Chantal spoke English well, with a minimal French accent.

Chantal refused a sherry too, and FBI agents weren't allowed to drink on duty, so we took that as our signal to fill our plates at one of the cafeteria lines before the POWs entered the mess tent.

More beef! Pot roast this time, with fresh onions, carrots and potatoes. And I couldn't resist a thick slab of chocolate cake. I didn't feel guilty, yet, about eating meals exempt from rationing, but as the prisoners of war took their place in the line once we were seated at our table, I began to feel a prickle of annoyance that they were eating so well. I wondered what our boys in German prisoner-of-war camps were having for dinner.

Now that I'd met several of the prisoners it was interesting to see them interact. Major Kapp, the SS flame tank commander we'd interviewed today, again sat at the head of the table nearest ours. A private who sat next to him spent much of his time refilling Kapp's water glass, lighting his cigarette and then getting him a cup of coffee. Once, when the private failed to strike a match immediately, Kapp turned an eye on him that chilled me, and I was sitting twenty feet away from him, guarded by MPs.

Bahnsen, the seminarian turned Luftwaffe navigator, sat as far away from Kapp as possible. His bruised face looked awful, and I saw him wince as he ate.

Chantal noticed Bahnsen too.

'What happened to that man?' he asked Rawlins.

'He said that he fell climbing into his bunk,' Rawlins said. 'But I understand that he was beaten by a couple of other prisoners. I couldn't get him to admit it.'

'That's unacceptable,' Chantal said.

Rawlins shrugged. 'That's his story and he's had plenty of opportunity to change it.'

'I'll need to question him, in private,' Chantal said.

'Of course, I'll arrange it,' Rawlins answered. 'But you'll be wasting your time. He won't want to tell you the truth; he'll just get beaten again.'

When we gathered for coffee in the officers' lounge I took Miss Osborne aside and told her what Steesen had said and then about the exchange between Chantal and Rawlins.

'If Kapp has the camp under such close control we must be very careful not to indicate which prisoners we think we might turn,' Miss Osborne said. 'We can't isolate them from the rest of the prisoners, not until we make our final decisions, so we can't protect them until then.'

'You think Bahnsen would be a likely recruit?' I asked.

'What do you think?' she asked.

Miss Osborne waited for my answer. I still wasn't used to being asked my opinion and I wanted to give her a reasoned reply.

'If the man was studying to be a Lutheran priest, and he's not a member of the Reich church, he can't be committed to the Nazi regime. And if Major Kapp had Bahnsen disciplined they must have had a conflict about something.'

Miss Osborne nodded. 'I agree,' she said. 'I think he's a good option for us. I just wish there was some way to protect him.'

Merle joined us in our barracks later for a drink from Miss Osborne's apparently bottomless flask of bourbon. She swallowed half her slug in one gulp.

'Miss Osborne,' I said, 'I'm just wondering, why don't you have a drink with the men before dinner?'

'Men don't take women seriously as it is. Men think they can hold their liquor and women can't. So I prefer to give them one less thing to diminish me with.'

'That's silly,' Merle said, holding out his cup for a refill. Miss Osborne poured him a generous slug.

'Is it?' she said. 'If a woman has two stiff drinks before dinner, and a man has two, what do you think of the woman, compared to the man?'

'Oh,' Merle said. 'Well, I guess I think that the woman is – I don't know.'

'Sloshed?'

'Yeah, I guess so.'

'Is the man?'

'Not after two drinks.'

'I'll have you know I can drink most men under the table,' she said. 'But I decline to do it.'

My admiration for Miss Osborne etched up yet another notch.

She threw back the rest of her bourbon. 'Now,' she said, 'let's talk about tomorrow. We'll be heading back to DC first thing in the morning.'

'Already?' I said.

'We've just been casing the joint, as you might say,' Miss Osborne said. 'Now we know who we have to deal with at the camp, and I don't mean just the prisoners. But we need to be better prepared for the rest of our interviews. Merle has a project to finish, a forged letter that needs to go on the plane to London on Friday. How long do you think it will take to finish it?'

'Half a day at the most,' Merle said.

'Good. Then I'd like you to spend the rest of tomorrow and Friday going over the prisoners' pay booklets. Do a short summary of each, on a separate page. If your writing is legible it doesn't need to be typed up.'

'Yes, ma'am,' he said.

'Louise, you and I will go through the prisoners' intake documents, the ones filled out at the holding centers in North Africa, and summarize each one. Between those and Merle's work we'll have a portrait of each prisoner, as we did for the five we interviewed today. We'll come back to Fort Meade Monday and, with luck, finish the rest of the interviews in a couple of weeks.'

We'd be in Washington for the weekend! I was going to see Joe if I had to hire Ellery Queen to track him down.

SEVEN

The air-raid siren squealed through the night, waking me from a sound sleep. I bolted upright, my heart pounding and my breathing short and shallow. Instinctively I threw myself under my bed.

Across the aisle I met Miss Osborne's eyes from her position on her stomach under her own bed.

'What was that?' Miss Osborne said.

'An air-raid warning?' I said.

'There haven't been any air raids in weeks,' she answered.

She was right. The United States had officially accepted the fact that the east coast was safe from air attack. The Germans didn't have even one aircraft carrier. No German aircraft could reach our eastern shores. Submarines were another matter entirely, but no one expected a German attack from the air anymore.

To save space in our luggage neither one of us had brought bathrobes, so we wrapped ourselves in sweaters and went outside to stand on the stoop. The screech of the siren stopped, then began to sound again in short spurts. Searchlights ranged all around us, but appeared to be coming from the watchtowers at the prisoner-of-war camp.

A couple of jeeps passed by, horns blasting, followed by a detachment of MPs, running hard toward the camp, some of them still buttoning their shirts and unholstering their side arms.

Merle appeared beside us, looking a bit disoriented but fully dressed. Miss Osborne grabbed his arm.

'Go find out what's happening,' she said. Merle nodded, and took off running himself.

'Do you think there's been an escape?' I asked.

'Maybe,' she answered. 'I can't imagine what else would cause this kind of ruckus.'

After about half an hour the siren stopped blasting and the searchlights ceased ranging about, focusing instead to the north of the camp. Miss Osborne and I sat on the steps to our quarters and waited. Merle trudged back to us, breathing hard.

'A POW escaped,' he said. 'They haven't caught him yet.'

He sat on a step below us to catch his breath.

'He's one of ours,' he added.

'What do you mean?' Miss Osborne asked.

'It's Hans Marek, the Pole, the one who tried to sell us souvenirs,' he answered. 'I talked to one of the guards. Marek shimmied up one of the supports of a watchtower and leapt over the stockade fences, both of them! It's a miracle he didn't break a leg.'

'Surely they'll pick him up right away,' I said.

Merle shrugged. 'He made it to the road, and he managed to steal a mess boy's white shirt, so there's nothing about him that identifies him as a prisoner. And it's dark as Hitler's soul out there.'

'Marek can't speak English!' Miss Osborne said. 'How far can he get?'

'True. The MP said they were calling Agent Williams. I reckon the FBI'll find him real soon.'

Agent Williams would be beside himself. He was sure every German POW was a potential saboteur. Pretty soon the area around Fort Meade would be crawling with G-men, bloodhounds and the Maryland state police. They'd find Marek.

We had breakfast at the camp officers' mess just outside the stockade, where we learned that Marek was still at large.

'He could be anywhere by now,' Lt Rawlins said, as he filled his plate with eggs and bacon. 'There's a Baltimore and Ohio Railroad spur about a mile from the camp. He could have hopped a freight train. They run all night.'

'What would he use for money?' Miss Osborne asked.

'He had the cash from selling all that German junk,' Rawlins said. 'Badges, cigarette lighters, ribbon bars. Half my soldiers were buying trinkets from him. Everyone wants a war souvenir.'

'It's shocking that Marek escaped so easily,' Merle said.

We'd set our trays down on a table near a window that faced the camp. The watchtower that guarded the front gate loomed overhead.

'This is just a barbed wire stockade.' Rawlins said. 'Not a state penitentiary.'

'But where could prisoners escape to? Most of them don't speak English,' Miss Osborne said, passing me cream for my coffee. 'Germany is an ocean away.'

'That's the FBI's problem now,' Rawlins said. 'I expect Agent Williams is more worried about what damage an escapee might do right here in this country.'

'Somehow I can't see Hans Marek as a saboteur,' Miss Osborne said.

'Me neither,' Rawlins said.

That wouldn't stop Williams from staging a full on manhunt if Hans Marek wasn't located soon.

Miss Osborne glanced at her watch. 'Mrs Pearlie, Mr Ellison, we need to be out front of the camp administration building, with our luggage, by eight. That's where the car will pick us up to take us back to Washington.'

'The car?' I asked.

'This morning's flights to Washington are full,' she said.

Thank God! If I was going to keep this job it looked like I would have to get accustomed to air travel, but I was still relieved to be avoiding it for now.

Instead Miss Osborne, Merle and I were crammed into the back seat of a Ford army sedan. A two-star general rode in the front next to the driver. He hadn't been pleased about giving us a lift, but made the best of it, tipping his cap to Miss Osborne and me and stowing his briefcase at his feet in the front seat. He didn't say a word to us on the short drive, leaving the three of us in the back to peer out the vehicle's narrow side windows at the scenery and whisper to each other. We were cramped and bored, but still I preferred that to watching the Maryland countryside slide by hundreds of feet below me!

The general dropped us off where Maryland Avenue crossed Constitution and we caught a crosstown bus, disembarking at the southern gate of the OSS compound.

'Stow your luggage in your offices, get some coffee and let's get to work,' Miss Osborne said to us.

If possible, the artists' workroom was even more chaotic than when we'd left it. There seemed to be a celebration of some kind going on.

'What's happened?' Merle asked.

A man with ink-stained fingers raised his coffee mug.

'The British have replaced their signposts and street signs!' he said. A cheer went up and we joined in happily. I knew from my previous work that Operation Sea Lion, the German plan for the invasion of Britain, had been postponed indefinitely, mostly because of the unexpectedly intense resistance of the British to the Blitz, and the German invasion of Russia. But it looked like Winston Churchill and his cabinet were confident there never would be a German invasion now. That meant that Great Britain would become the landing stage for an Allied invasion of Europe. We could pack the country with Yanks and military equipment until the time came to move on to the European mainland. I hoped the Brits were prepared for our invasion of their little island.

We dropped Merle off at his office to complete his forged letter and went on to Miss Osborne's office, where we unpacked the prisoner-of-war intake papers Lt Rawlins had given us.

'We have fifty-eight documents,' Miss Osborne said, 'including those of the two men who disappeared over the side of the ship.' The prisoners had been processed at either Oran or Casablanca before they'd been loaded on a ship bound for the States.

'OK,' Miss Osborne said, 'let's alphabetize these first, then begin reading and summarizing. A page per prisoner, please. Handwritten is fine, as long as it's readable.'

After a few hours we'd waded through a third of the prisoners' documents. It was slow going. The forms had been completed by dozens of American soldiers, some with terrible handwriting, who didn't speak German. Translators must have been scarce. One prisoner's form I came upon was filled only with question marks!

* * *

I ran into Merle on my way out of the Que tempo to pick up a sandwich at a café across the street. I just wasn't in the mood to deal with the crowd and commotion at the OSS cafeteria.

'Want to join me for lunch?' I said to him.

'Yes, please,' he answered. 'I finished that letter and got it sent off to London. But I have a shocking headache. I need someplace quiet.'

We found a table for two in the back of a tiny lunch counter, where we ordered grilled pimento cheese sandwiches and French fries. I had milk, but Merle asked for coffee. It was late for lunch so we had the place to ourselves.

'This is the best cure for a headache,' he said, 'coffee and aspirin.' He tossed back two tablets with his first gulp. 'How are your summaries coming along?'

'Slowly,' I said. 'But we should be done by the end of the day tomorrow.'

'I should be finished reading the prisoners' paybooks too,' Merle answered. 'I hope so, anyway. I want the weekend off before we go back to Fort Meade.'

Once our plates were cleared and we'd both ordered coffee, Merle leaned toward me and whispered.

'Look at this. I bought it off Hans Marek.' He reached into his pocket and pulled out a German cigarette lighter and handed it to me. The lighter's case was embossed with a skull and crossbones, the Nazi SS death's head.

I dropped the lighter on the table. 'That is revolting,' I said. 'I can't believe you'd want to own such a nasty thing.'

'Come on, Louise, this lighter is history! I can pass this down to my grandkids someday.'

'How much did you pay for it?' I asked.

'Ten bucks,' he said. 'A real deal! One of the fellows at the office has already offered me fifteen for it!'

'So part of the money Marek will spend during his escape came from you,' I said. 'How do you know he's not planning to derail a train or something?'

'You know that if I hadn't bought it someone else would have. And Marek had pockets full of other stuff to sell. The guards and MPs were all buying things from him.'

I drained my milk, left a dollar bill and a quarter on the table for the tab and tip and collected my sweater and hat. 'I'll see you later,' I said.

'Don't go off angry.'

'I'm not, I've got work to do.'

Once out of the lunchroom I waited at the crosswalk for a break in the traffic so I could get across 23rd Street. Fuming, I'd left the lunch counter quickly so as not to lose my temper with Merle. I had to work with the man. And I knew hundreds of American soldiers and others were stripping German prisoners of whatever they could – side arms, SS daggers and Iron Crosses were the most prized – as mementos of their participation in a historic conflict. It was against all rules of warfare and the Geneva Convention, and I thought it was cheap and petty. Like robbing corpses, only worse, because the victims were alive to experience their degradation.

I found myself wondering if the SS lighter Marek had sold Merle had belonged to Major Kapp, but somehow I doubted that haughty officer would stoop to selling his personal possessions, even through an intermediary, to buy a couple of candy bars at the camp PX. By the time I'd gotten to Miss Osborne's office I'd calmed down. My anger wasn't going to stop anyone from stealing from German prisoners, or corpses, and I knew that my energy could be better used doing my job.

By quitting time Miss Osborne and I had plowed through another twenty sets of German prisoner intake forms. We'd learned that the two German Czechs who'd disappeared overboard while crossing the Atlantic had not only lived at the same address and vanished aboard ship on the same day, but had been conscripted on the same day too.

'That's three coincidences,' I said to Miss Osborne.

'But not impossible,' Miss Osborne answered. 'The Germans are very organized. I can see German conscription officials proceeding block by block.'

'But dying on the same day too? And if they did commit suicide, that's even odder.'

'Maybe they were sitting on the deck rail together and got washed overboard,' she said.

Miss Osborne saw my disbelieving expression.

'I don't think so either,' she said. 'It's too outlandish to believe. We have enough to do without Pinkertoning these men's deaths, but I can't help but wonder if they were murdered by one of the POWs we're interviewing. I wish we knew the answer to that question. I'd like to know if we recruit a killer to our mission.'

I dropped my valise on the floor and my hat on the hall table, too tired to tackle the stairs to my bedroom yet. I'd gotten little sleep last night because of the prisoner escape, then spent a claustrophobic hour squished in the back of an army staff car between Miss Osborne and Merle, followed by a full workday deciphering prisoner intake forms, every one written in a different handwriting and most incomplete. But I was thrilled, because my day was much more interesting than any day I had spent in the Registry, and I hoped I'd have many more away from a typewriter and a file cabinet!

I riffled through the mail on the hall table. Nothing for me. That was both good and bad. I loved my parents and my brother, but their letters just reminded me of how badly I did not want to return to Wilmington, North Carolina to live in my parents' house and work at the family fish camp. And be pushed by my mother into a second marriage to anyone who could support me.

I was nervous about my future. Like all war workers my contract was for the duration of the war and no more. But I wanted to continue to earn my living in either Washington or another city, to have my own apartment and maybe even a car someday. Now that I was more than a file clerk I intended to acquire the skills and connections that would help me stay employed after the war was over.

The government was already preparing working women to lose their war jobs and return to their traditional domestic role. All the women's magazines were full of advertisements for how to use the cash we'd get from selling our bonds after the war was over, and it wasn't for education. Most suggested down payments on houses, sets of fine china or silver, whatever might be needed to set up a home. All that was required was a husband, and I didn't have one.

My savings – and I planned to add my raise to them – would go toward college if I couldn't find a decent job after the war. A woman I admired greatly in the Research and Analysis branch where I'd first worked had offered to sponsor me for Smith College if I wanted to go.

I continued flipping through the mail, looking for a Malta postmark without success. I wished I heard more often from Rachel, my Jewish friend who escaped with her two children from France at the last possible moment before being sent to a labor camp. I hoped some of my unauthorized work on her behalf had helped her get to Malta. She was safe there, but I still loved hearing from her.

There was nothing from Joe, either. Damn the man! He'd popped up here Monday night without any notice, been spoiled and feted by all of us, hinted around at the chance he and I might be able to spend some time together alone, then took off without leaving me his address or phone number! Yes, we didn't want anyone to know about our romance. But how hard would it have been for him to mail me a note telling me how to get in touch with him?

I picked up my valise and my hat and stomped upstairs to my room to unpack and clean up. I'd had a wonderfully long hot shower at our billet last night, so I just sponged off and changed into trousers and a checked shirt and cardigan. I drew open my underwear drawer and pulled out a half-pint, close to empty, of Gordon's gin, filled a tumbler with what I judged to be about a jigger, waved a bit of vermouth over it, took two aspirin and chased it with a swallow of the martini. Sitting on my bed, supported by two pillows at my back, I sipped my martini with closed eyes, feeling the ache in the back of my neck fade away.

'Welcome home,' Milt said, as he pulled the dining room chair out for me, then deftly helped me push myself up to the dining room table, all with just one arm.

'How did I do?' he asked.

'Very well,' I said.

Milt seated his mother, then he and Henry took their seats. Ada was missing from the dinner table again tonight. I wished she was here so I couldn't postpone telling her that I had no way of finding out if her German husband was a prisoner of war. At least, I knew he wasn't at Fort Meade. Why had I said I would try to find out if Rein was a prisoner of war? Just to get her to calm down and go to bed the night she woke me up so I could go back to sleep? For that selfish act I was sentenced to another emotional meeting with her, and I wanted to get it over with as soon as possible.

I was back on rations. Phoebe, Milt, Ada, Henry and I had agreed that we'd rather have meatless meals than eat beef tongue or brains, so tonight we had macaroni and cheese, green beans, carrots, fresh rolls and sliced peaches for dessert. There was margarine instead of butter for the rolls, since Dellaphine had used up our week's ration of butter to make Joe's cake. Which made me remember how angry I was with him!

'So,' Phoebe said to me, 'how was your time away?'

I felt Henry's eyes on me. He had to be curious why a government girl, just a file clerk, needed to leave town for her job.

'It was fine,' I said.

'Do you have a new job?' Henry said.

'Not really,' I answered. 'There's a shortage of experienced clerical workers, you know.'

'Lending you out, are they?' Henry asked.

'Cut it out,' Milt said to him. 'You know she can't say anything.'

Henry shrugged.

Since the topic had been broached I decided to go all in. 'I may be traveling quite a bit,' I said. 'It looks like I'll be out of town all next week. Maybe the following week too.'

Phoebe put her fork down on her plate, wiped her mouth and glared at me. 'In my day a girl didn't travel for work. It would ruin her reputation.'

'We're at war, Mother,' Milt said. 'Louise can take care of herself.'

'If you're about to tell me that times are changing, I'm well aware of it,' Phoebe said to her son. 'That doesn't mean I approve.' She turned back to me. 'Does your mother know about this?'

I was thirty years old and a widow, for God's sake! And shacked up with a foreign refugee, which I planned to continue to be if I ever got Joe's address and phone number. But of course I kept my annoyance to myself.

'Phoebe,' I said. 'I appreciate your concern. I assure you that I am perfectly safe when I travel.' Then I glared at Henry. 'Yes, my job has changed somewhat, but you know darn well I can't talk about it. You're only quizzing me because I'm a woman. If I were a man you wouldn't think twice about me going out of town for work.'

'She's got you there,' Milt said, chuckling, as he carefully used the side of his fork to cut a slippery canned peach into bite-sized chunks.

We finished our so-called dessert in silence.

Phoebe and I carried the dishes into the kitchen, where Dellaphine was already up to her elbows in suds and Madeleine was finishing her own dinner at the kitchen table. Phoebe loaded the coffee things on to a tray to take into the lounge and took it out into the hall.

Madeline carefully folded her napkin so it could be used again, and grinned at me. Of course she and Dellaphine had overheard the entire dinner table conversation. 'Mr Henry just wants to know why you have a job that takes you out of town and he doesn't,' Madeleine said. 'He's worried you're more important than he is.' I saw her glance at her mother's back to make sure Dellaphine wasn't watching, then take a small square of paper out of her pocket and hand it to me, her finger up to her mouth to shush me.

It was from Joe. All the note said was 'Meet me at Martin's Tavern, Georgetown, Saturday, one o'clock'. He'd signed it with just a 'J'.

I heard the sound of Dellaphine turning from the sink and jammed my hand with the note into my dress pocket, my blood pounding through my heart so strongly I could feel it hammering on my ribs. Dellaphine went into the pantry, and Madeleine leaned toward me and whispered, 'Mr Joe met me at the bus stop and gave the note to me to bring to you.' Dellaphine came back into the kitchen with a clean dishtowel. I mouthed a 'thank you' to Madeleine before heading to the staircase.

'Aren't you going to join us, Louise?' Phoebe called out from the lounge.

'No, ma'am,' I answered back. 'I'm tired. I'm going to read in bed.'

Which I did. I read Joe's note over and over again. He was a smart man. Devious might be a better word; his spycraft was worthy of one of our agents. He'd written me a note that didn't include his address or telephone number, arranging for us to meet at a restaurant we'd never been to before in an unfamiliar part of town, during an innocent time of day, all without actually identifying himself. And delivered said note to me by meeting our cook's daughter at her bus stop. Madeleine was a perfect go-between for us, because I didn't tell her mother about her late Saturday nights at 'U' Street jazz joints, so we could hold each other's private life hostage.

I jerked awake. I'd fallen asleep fully dressed, *The Robe* open on my lap, when I heard the sound of the front door closing. Ada wasn't being very quiet. I was glad she'd woken me up, though; I was desperate to talk to her about her husband. I heard her coming up the stairs and called out to her as softly as I could while still getting her attention.

'Ada?'

She heard me and came straight into my room, closing the door behind her and sitting on the corner of my bed. She was dressed beautifully, as she always was when she went out with one of her many admirers. Cleavage had come back in style, and she'd been quick to buy dresses that highlighted her best feature. Her hair was dressed in the newest style too, pressed smoothly back into a knot at the base of her neck with a sequined half-hat perched on top of her head, tied under the knot with a ribbon. Ada was a party girl, and went out most nights with either her fellow band members or some man who'd picked her up after a set.

'Have you found out anything about Rein?' she asked, her voice low.

'I'm sorry, nothing at all. It turns out I just don't have that kind of access,' I said.

She buried her head in her hands.

'I don't think I can live like this,' she said, looking up at me, her eye shadow smeared down her cheeks.

I felt so terribly sorry for her. I took her shaking shoulders in my hands and forced her to sit up straight.

'Listen,' I said, 'you mustn't worry so. You'll make yourself ill. It's so unlikely that your husband will wind up in a prisoner-of-war camp in the States. And why would he reveal his marriage to you? You haven't heard from him in, what, four years?'

'So I'm to hope he's simply forgotten about me, that he doesn't still despise me for refusing to live in Germany with him?'

'Yes, why not? He's a Luftwaffe pilot, a big shot, he may be a colonel by now. He's probably surrounded by dozens of Wintergarten showgirls when he's in Berlin. Heck, maybe he's divorced you in Germany, have you ever thought of that?'

'What a lovely thought,' she said. 'But you didn't know Rein. He won't forget that I rejected him.'

I decided to change the subject.

'Who did you go out with tonight? Did you have fun?'

Ada shrugged. 'Some middle-aged fellow. I think Bert was his name. He came up to me after my last set and asked me to go to Sans Souci with him. And no, it wasn't much fun. He was some kind of salesman. I can't remember what he sold though, something the army buys a lot of.'

'Condoms?'

Ada actually laughed then. 'No, I would have remembered that!'

'Go on and get some sleep,' I said. 'You can't do anything about Rein, so there's no point in worrying about him.'

'Easy for you to say,' Ada said, easing off my bed. 'You're

not looking at the inside of a German-American detention camp.'

I got ready for bed and climbed in, turning off my bedside light after sticking a bookmark in *The Robe*. I put Ada out of my mind. There was nothing I could do for her except keep her secret.

Merle and I met with Miss Osborne in her office the next morning.

'Merle,' Miss Osborne said, 'can you finish reviewing the rest of the paybooks today?'

'Yes, ma'am,' he said. 'Easily.'

'And the two of us,' she said, turning to me, 'we can finish summarizing the prisoners' papers by noon, don't you think?'

'Yes,' I said. 'So many of them are incomplete anyway.'

She nodded. 'Then let's meet back here about three o'clock to get organized for our trip to Fort Meade on Monday. Now, I expect we'll need to be there a full week, so pack accordingly, but still as lightly as possible. I don't know if we can catch an airplane flight or not.'

Merle, who'd been sitting on the corner of Miss Osborne's desk, hopped to the floor, ready to go to his office.

'Oh, wait, I almost forgot to tell you,' Miss Osborne said. 'The FBI caught Marek, the escaped Polish prisoner, last night.'

'Where?' I said. 'How far did he get?'

'Baltimore,' she said. 'He was at a brothel.'

'No kidding!' Merle said.

'He tried to pass himself as a Dutch refugee, but the girl he was with noticed the Iron Cross tattooed on his bicep and called the police. He had a bag full of strudel from the bakery down the street with him.'

'So he spent his take from selling Nazi souvenirs on food and girls,' I said. Agent Williams would be disappointed, I thought, not to find fuses and plastic explosives on Marek. There was no glory in capturing a man starving for strudel and a woman.

By noon Miss Osborne and I were finished with our work. She looked at her watch and shuffled through some papers on her desk. I knew she was thinking about what other business we could complete before meeting Merle at three o'clock. This was my chance.

'Miss Osborne,' I said.

'Yes,' she answered, looking up at me.

'About the two men who were murdered, Muntz and Aach. I know you're concerned about their deaths. Whether or not they were murdered, I mean.'

Miss Osborne intertwined her hands and pursed her lips.

'Yes,' she said. 'I am. Very. If they were murdered it could impact our operation negatively, for two reasons. First, the prisoners of war could be intimidated by knowing that there's a killer in the camp. Depending on who it is, and why the murders were done, they might be reluctant to volunteer for our operation for fear of reprisal. Then there's the possibility that we might unknowingly recruit this killer for our operation, and I don't like the possibilities there. The man might run for his life when he lands in Italy, or inform the Germans about our black propaganda operation. Our work is so important to winning the war, we have to find the right people to send.'

'Ma'am,' I said, 'I've got a few hours until we need to meet Merle. Why don't I go over to the Registry and search the files for information on these two men? I could find my way around the place in a blackout. Since I don't work there anymore I'd need a note from you, but once I present it no one will question me. I know everyone. I'd have full access to the files, the Reading Room, the Map Room, even the telephone directory archive.'

At this she smiled at me. 'You're going to look up their telephone numbers?'

'All right, that was silly, but you don't know what I might be able to find out. What if these two were in contact with a resistance group, or had some other strategic value? And then there's Reichenberg itself. I know it's a long shot, but we keep noticing that the two men lived at the same address. What do we know about Reichenberg? Maybe Muntz and Aach lived next door to a munitions factory, or something that would suggest a motive for their murder. I know I'm exaggerating, but it's just a few hours.'

'That's a very long shot,' she said.

'I know.'

'OK,' she said, 'you're right, it's worth a try. What should I say in the note you need?'

When I presented Miss Osborne's note to my old boss, Jesse Shera, he read it and then handed it back to me. 'Pick up a visitor's pass, and make sure you return it at the end of the day. Use whatever you need, God knows you know your way around here.'

It felt odd to find myself back at the Registry, the Central Information Division of OSS. I'd only left it a few days ago, but mentally I felt as though I'd been gone a year. I took in the immense archive crammed with row upon row of wooden file cabinets and index files containing the vast knowledge collected by the scholars of the Research and Analysis branch of OSS. Need to find out the gauge of railroad tracks in Algeria? You could find it here. Or where pre-war Mercedes-Benz automobile production plants were located in Germany? Want a tourist guide to Italy to mine for cultural information to educate the Allied troops that would occupy it? It was neatly tucked away under 'Italy, Travel Guides, Pre-war'.

For the first year and a half of my life in Washington DC I spent my days indexing, filing and distributing all that knowledge to the people who needed it, from the President to soldiers in the field. It was work important to the war effort, but boring and pedestrian. I was so happy to be away from it.

I'd forgotten how much my fingertips could hurt after an hour flipping through index cards and file folders. Muntz and Aach weren't listed in our files anywhere. They weren't journalists, or avant-garde artists, or aristocrats, or Jews, or Communists, or wealthy playboys, or resistance members. Neither of them had ever contacted an Allied agent. No newspaper or magazine clippings mentioned them. Neither had graduated from a German university recently. And yes, I checked the Reichenberg telephone book. It was an old one, from 1939, that looked like it had had an entire pot of coffee spilled on it, but neither man had a listing.

Muntz and Aach were nobodies. Just two young Czech men, ethnic Germans, who were drafted into the Wehrmacht and died mysteriously on the *Abel Stoddard*, ferrying prisoners of war to the United States, damn it.

Now to get familiar with Reichenberg, which had its own hefty file. I lugged it over to a free spot at a table in the Reading Room. The space was just as I remembered it. Industrial ceiling lights struggled to illuminate the tables through the fug of cigarette smoke that floated over them. Maps of the world's war zones wallpapered the room. Files, pencils, papers and overfilled ashtrays crowded the tables. Mostly men, most in uniform, pored over stacks of files looking for buried gems of information that might have some strategic value. Clerks, mostly girls, hovered around the tables, collecting request slips and ferrying discarded files back to the file rooms.

I slid into a hard wooden chair and shook papers, photographs, clippings and pamphlets out of the Reichenberg file. Reichenberg was located in the northern tip of the Sudetenland. It had been the capital of Bohemia, a province of Czechoslovakia. It wasn't far from Dresden and was inhabited by ethnic Germans. In fact the city had been the unofficial capital of German Czechoslovakia.

No one could say that the Sudetenland had resisted German annexation. The recession had devastated its industries. Hitler offered the Germans who lived there the same prosperity he'd brought to the Reich, with the added advantage of being part of a powerful, successful German state. European leaders like Neville Chamberlain were eager to appease Hitler. Czechoslovakia's protests were ignored. Between the first and the tenth of December 1938 the Sudetenland became part of the Reich without a shot being fired. Reichenberg became the capital of the new German province of Reichstag Sudetenland.

By March of 1939 what was left of Czechoslovakia had been conquered and occupied by the Nazis. And my lover, Joe Prager, was teaching Slavic languages at the University of London at the time, or so he said.

I borrowed a magnifying glass from the army captain sitting next to me and examined the dozen or so photographs included in the file. Reichenberg's buildings were typically Eastern European, thick and bulky, at the most twenty stories or so tall, constructed in baroque or neoclassical styles. Nazi flags flew from the tallest buildings. There weren't many cars, but a few horses pulled wagons through the streets. Tram tracks ran down the center of the main streets. One photograph was of a group of German officers, several of whom were SS, lounging on the steps of an official-looking building. I inspected the officers' faces, but recognized no one from the Fort Meade camp.

The few newspaper clippings came from American newspapers that reported on the Sudetenland crisis. One described an exodus of the Jewish population when German armed forces occupied the city. Another showed the burned out ruins of Reichenberg's synagogue, torched during *Kristallnacht*. There was nothing remarkable in anything I read.

Until I reached the last paper in the sheaf that had been contained in the file. It was a page from a Reichenberg newspaper, with the date November 3, 1933, at the top. What I saw just about singed my eyebrows.

When I grew up in Wilmington, North Carolina, there were just two definitions of sex. Until marriage sex was holding hands and stealing kisses on the porch swing of a girl's parents' house. After marriage sex was conducted quickly in the missionary position. My late husband, Bill, and I found married life quite exciting, but then we didn't know anything else.

When I arrived in Washington early in 1942 to work as a government girl I discovered that men and women could have unmarried sex without being tarred and feathered and ridden out of town on a rail, although girls could still lose their reputations, jobs and lodging if it became public knowledge. I also learned that some men could love men and some women could love women without the earth cracking open beneath them and dumping them instantly into the flames of hell. What with drinking martinis, going to jazz clubs and opening a charge account, I considered myself quite worldly these days.

But my confidence in my sophistication faded when I saw the half-page advertisement for a Reichenberg nightclub. I couldn't read the German text, but the heading showed a martini glass with a tiger cub curled around it, his cat's eyes entranced by the hedonism that unfolded in the photograph below.

And what a spectacle it was. The nightclub, lit by extravagant gas chandeliers, was jammed with partygoers wearing sparkling evening gowns and wide-lapelled tuxedos, flourishing cigarette holders and champagne glasses. At the corner of a long polished bar, backed with a mirror that reflected row after row of liquor bottles, a crowd of young men, their hair slicked flat over their foreheads, played cards, a stack of paper money piled in the middle of the table. A blonde woman wearing a tiara, with a skirt slit halfway up her thigh, sat on the other end of the bar, flirting with three men who surrounded her. In the foreground a small orchestra made up of colored men dressed in white tails played for a dozen or so dancing couples. The orchestra was a long way from home. The name displayed on its drum set was 'Savannah's Finest Jazz'.

In the background of the photograph I could see an opulent stage with performers posed on it. Using my trusty borrowed magnifying glass I peered at the performers, beautiful young men and women, heavily made up and without a stitch of clothing on above their waists, being ogled by a crowd of men and women who clustered below the stage. Under the scrutiny of the magnifying glass it was clear that some of the oglers in evening gowns were men and some of the tuxedos were worn by women.

What struck me the most about the photograph was the look of abandon and pleasure on the participants' faces. No one cowered in a corner. Not one of them was afraid. Of being recognized, of losing a job or a home. I'd heard plenty about the wild cabaret culture of pre-war Germany, but this was the first time I'd seen it illustrated. When I returned the magnifying glass to my neighbor I hoped he didn't notice the heat rising on my neck and cheeks.

I shoved the items from the file back into its folders, embarrassed that I'd been so distracted by the nightclub ad. Now that the Nazis were in power in Reichenberg I doubted the club was still there.

When I left the Reading Room I tossed the Reichenberg file on to the return table. So far I had learned nothing of our two dead prisoners of war.

After Pearl Harbor, as the nation geared up for war in Europe and the Pacific, the United States government sent out a request to the entire country for the printed materials that could help us win the war. If you were an economics professor and had a collection of German textbooks Uncle Sam asked you to mail them to the government right away. If you owned foreign journals, magazines or newspapers your uncle wanted those too. Been on holiday overseas recently? Send the OSS your guidebooks, maps and postcards. It was no exaggeration to say that the best map resources available to our military when the war started were the maps included in the *National Geographic Magazine*.

The public responded. When I first visited the OSS Map Room months ago donated maps filled the center of its workroom in a pile that must have been ten feet high. Clerks opened the mail and tossed donated maps on to the pile, and more clerks grabbed the nearest map and cataloged and filed it. The indexed collection now held a half-million sheets, all neatly tucked away and easily found.

The young man at the map reference desk was so short and slight I had a good view of the top of his head. There was a height requirement for military service and I was pretty sure he didn't reach it.

'Yes, ma'am?' he asked.

'I need a map—' I began.

'Really,' he said, waving his arm about the room. 'Well, since this is the Map Room, you've come to the right place.'

'Don't be short with me,' I said. 'I'm not having the best day.'

'Me neither. Sorry. What are you looking for?'

'I need a city map of Reichenberg, Germany. Used to be in Czechoslovakia.'

'I know it. Near Dresden. Let me look.'

He vanished through a door behind the desk. I could see rows of metal shelves filled with file boxes before he closed the door behind him.

A few minutes later he came back to the desk with a folded map. I had Muntz and Aach's address written on my notepad and I drew it out of my pocketbook in anticipation. The clerk unfolded the map on top of the counter and my enthusiasm vanished.

'Oh, no,' I said. 'This is nothing like what I need.'

The map laid out before me must once have hung on a Czech schoolroom wall. It showed most of Bohemia, with a circle representing Reichenberg plunked in the middle of it, surrounded by garish illustrations that represented the area's industries – textiles, glassblowing and papermaking. The circle that represented the city was dominated by a purple cathedral and a statue of some hero perched on a horse. In the country-side a couple of cows and a goat grazed contentedly in fields that held a haystack or two. There wasn't even a road marked on the map, much less a street.

'This won't work,' I said. 'I need a city map, with the streets marked. Or an *A to Z.*'

'I'm sorry,' he said. 'This is all I got.'

'OK, thanks,' I answered, shoving my notepad back into my pocketbook.

I'd hoped to be able to pinpoint the location of our two dead prisoners' address, but that was impossible now. If there wasn't a map of the city here there wasn't one anywhere in North America.

I checked my watch. I had forty-five minutes before I was to meet with Miss Osborne and Merle back at the MO branch. Maybe time enough for a personal errand. An unauthorized personal errand. I wasn't sure where to start looking, but since 'prisoners' started with a 'p' I headed for the 'P' files. The aisle was dim, lit only by the green-shaded lamps on top of the file cabinets, but I didn't turn on the overhead light, hoping to retain some anonymity. I opened a file drawer and began to flip through it, feeling soreness returning to my fingertips again.

'Returning to the scene of your crimes, I see,' a voice said just a few feet from me. I hadn't heard anyone approaching and, fearing the voice belonged to someone who might report me, I slammed the file drawer closed. On my left hand.

'The devil!' I said, cradling my hand. I turned to see who had interrupted me.

It was Ruth (thank you, Jesus). 'You scared me to death, sneaking up on me!' I said.

Ruth took my left hand and felt all its fingers, one by one. 'I don't think you've broken anything,' she said. 'But that hand will ache tomorrow. I'm sorry I startled you. What are you doing here?'

'Research for my new job,' I said. Ruth and I had worked together in the files until I'd moved to the MO branch. The woman was a filing machine. She could file twice as fast as any of the clerks and had the memory of an elephant. She looked just like always. A Mount Holyoke graduate, she wore makeup and pearls even when dressed in a smock and trousers.

'How is the new job?' she asked.

'I like it so far.'

'Can I help you find something?' she asked.

'I'm looking for a list of German prisoners of war in the United States,' I said.

Now I was committed. I had no one's request or permission to look for Rein Hermann's name in the OSS files, but I was going to do it anyway. Ruth would assume I had a good reason for my search, and she wouldn't mention it to anyone. She helped dozens of people find files every day.

'I bet you expected to find it under "Prisoners of War, German", didn't you? You know better than that. Come with me,' Ruth said.

Ruth led me to a separate bank of file cabinets in a corner of the archive, away from the reception desk and Shera's office, I was glad to see.

'These are files that are so active we keep them here to make it easy to add files quickly,' she said. 'This cabinet contains the prisoner-of-war lists by camp name.'

Luckily for me most of the file jackets were empty, since few prisoners had arrived stateside yet. It took no time at all for me to look through the alphabetized lists. Rein Hermann's name wasn't there. Yet, anyway. I could ease Ada's nerves for now.

I'd missed lunch but was due back at the MO office soon. I stopped by the OSS snack bar on my way back to the Que tempo and bought a package of peanut butter crackers and a Coke. That would have to hold me until dinner tonight.

Sitting on a stone wall in the middle of the OSS campus I choked down the crackers and Coke. I was disappointed that I hadn't found any information about the two German men who died crossing the Atlantic on their way to Fort Meade, but I knew beforehand that was unlikely. I'd really hoped to find a city map of Reichenberg too, so I could locate where Muntz and Aach lived. It seemed to me that it was important somehow that the two men lived at the same address and I was terribly curious about their neighborhood.

But I had a new idea, one I didn't plan to ask Miss Osborne's permission to implement. Joe was Czech, and when I saw him I'd share the story of the two dead German prisoners of war with him and ask him what he knew about Reichenberg. I thought I knew Miss Osborne well enough now to be sure she wouldn't want me to talk to anyone outside OSS about this. But I was also sure that if I brought her usable information she would be glad to have it and excuse me for involving Joe to get it. At least I hoped so.

Merle and I drank coffee and waited an hour for Miss Osborne to appear in the conference room. She flew in with her coffee in one hand and a stapler in another.

'Sorry,' she said, 'I had to approve some "black" materials we're flying to London tonight. Good work on your letter, Merle.'

Merle nodded his thanks.

'Merle,' she continued, 'Louise had a couple of spare hours

after lunch, so she went to the Registry to see if she could learn anything about the two prisoners of war that went overboard while crossing the Atlantic to the States. Anything, Louise?'

'Nothing,' I said. 'Muntz and Aach weren't referenced at all. And I looked everywhere. Even in a 1939 Reichenberg telephone book. I found a file on Reichenberg itself, but there was nothing unexpected in it. I hunted for a city map too, hoping to pinpoint our deceased prisoners' neighborhood, but the Map Room didn't have one.'

'That's too bad,' she said. 'So we have nothing to add to the information we already have about them?'

'No, ma'am.'

'Well, you tried. Let's put our curiosity about these men aside for the moment. You have the rest of the summaries, both Merle's and ours?'

'Yes,' I said, putting my hands on the two stacks of papers.

'Now,' she said. 'We need to merge and alphabetize these. Please use the stapler. I despise paperclips.'

The three of us shuffled paper for an hour. When we were finished we had an organized description of the population of German prisoners of war at Fort Meade. After we'd returned the prisoners' intake papers and paybooks to the camp headquarters we would work from our own summaries.

The last thing Miss Osborne did was to locate the summaries for each of the men we had already interviewed and attach my interview notes to them. I noticed that Miss Osborne also flagged the summaries for Muntz and Aach, the men who had disappeared off the *Abel Stoddard*.

'Louise,' she said to me, 'I expect you to guard these documents with your life. There are no copies. I'll commandeer a briefcase of some kind you can use to carry them. If it wouldn't attract so much attention I'd handcuff the case to your wrist!'

'I will take good care of them,' I said, drawing the mound of paper toward me. I well understood the importance of our notes. From these men we might recruit the first operatives who would carry 'black' propaganda behind German lines in northern Italy.

I left the stack of papers on the seat of my office chair and shoved it under my desk. Miss Osborne had given me a key to my office, and for the first time since I'd started this new job I locked the door after I left.

EIGHT

Billy Martin's Tavern was a squat brick building, painted white, in the middle of Georgetown. Narrow-paned windows framed with black shutters pierced the second floor. A narrow roof sheltered the entrance from the weather. I'd heard of the Tavern, of course, but had never been there.

I was early for my date with Joe, so I waited around the corner of the building. I didn't want him to find me already seated at a table, on my third glass of iced tea; he might think I was desperate to see him. Which I was, but I didn't want it to be obvious.

Georgetown was once a town in its own right, set down at the highest navigable point up the Potomac next to Rock Creek Park. It was named 'Georgetown, DC,' and stayed independent until the Washington and Georgetown horse car company made travel between the capital city and the little port easier. That, plus the silting up of canals and the Potomac, sealed Georgetown's fate, and it became a small but colorful Washington neighborhood. It was old and historic, and as I looked around I was charmed by its tiny stone houses and quaint shops.

I idly watched an old Buick pull up to the front of the Tavern and park, and was startled to see Joe and another man get out of the car. I'd expected him to come on foot from the bus stop and I prayed he didn't see me holding up an alley wall of the Tavern.

The two men went inside and I waited for my breathing to return to normal before I collected myself and breezed inside. Inside the Tavern was dark, lit by hanging lamps with Tiffany-style shades and dim wall sconces that did little to light the gloom created by mahogany paneling, the long mahogany bar and the dark wood tables and booths. What a perfect meeting place for secret lovers!

Joe and his companion had taken seats on one side of a booth. When Joe saw me he beckoned me over. Both men stood up and then Joe kissed me, so sweetly I instantly forgave him for all his past and future mistakes. Slightly dizzy from the kiss, I managed to slide in to the hard bench of the booth. The two men sat down after me.

'Louise, this is my roommate, Ken Tutterow,' he said. 'I wanted you two to meet.'

'Ma'am,' Ken said, 'I need to leave for home shortly, but I wanted at least to meet you. Joe talks about you with such admiration.' Tutterow was well into his sixties, I guessed, maybe almost seventy. Grey hair circled a prominent bald spot. His warm smile revealed a narrow gap between his front teeth.

I felt myself blushing at his words. 'Well, it's very nice to meet you too.' I said.

'You,' Ken said to Joe, 'I will see Sunday night.'

After Ken left Joe took his seat again and reached across the tabletop for my hand.

'He seems like a nice man,' I said.

'He's doing good work,' Joe said, 'implementing the Lanham Act.'

'Thank God something is finally being done about child care,' I said. 'Have you seen those awful stories in the newspapers about little children chained inside trailer homes or even locked in cars outside factories all day while their mothers work? There aren't enough day nurseries or relatives to care for them.'

The Lanham Act allocated funds to local communities to build and staff their own day nurseries. The nurseries were open to everyone and heavily subsidized, so poor women could use them too.

'Ken didn't need to take me in, either, he can afford the apartment rent on his own. I was looking for another boarding house, which I didn't think I could bear, considering our situation, and he instantly offered to share his place with me.'

'I'm so glad to see you,' I said, squeezing his hand.

'I'm sorry about Monday night,' he said, 'showing up like

that at Phoebe's without any notice. I was sort of stuck. You handled it brilliantly, though.'

'It was a shock,' I said, 'but Joe, we just cannot let Phoebe know about us. She's so old-fashioned, she might evict me. And my job depends on my security clearance.'

'I understand. It's that suspicious Slav accent of mine.'

A waiter stopped by our table and seemed irritated that we hadn't looked at the menu yet. We ordered drinks, a Coke for me and coffee for Joe. We had to release each other's hands to look at the menu.

'They serve a lot of seafood here,' Joe said. 'I know you don't like fish, but they have other dishes too.'

'I'll be fine,' I said. I'd be willing to eat jellied eels as long as I sat across the table from Joe.

When the waiter returned I ordered Brunswick stew, which I hadn't had since I'd left North Carolina. Joe requested a fried oyster sandwich and fries.

'So,' I said, after the waiter had picked up the menus and walked away, 'why are you back in Washington so soon?' I lowered my voice. 'Are you still working for the JDC?'

Joe closed his eyes for a second and winced, as if he'd had a stab of pain. It frightened me and I reached for his hand.

'Are you all right?' I asked.

'Yes, I'm still working for the JDC,' he said, looking directly at me again. 'We lost one of our people in Lisbon. Murdered. He was shot in the back while having a coffee in Rossio Square.'

'Oh, no!'

'Yes. Anyway, I'm taking the place of the man they're sending to Portugal to replace him.'

Consciously we talked for the rest of the meal about anything but the war. The weather was cooling off quickly, so Joe planned to borrow Phoebe's car to get his winter clothes from the boarding house attic, where he'd stored them when he went to New York City. We both badly wanted to see the new movie *For Whom the Bell Tolls*. Starring Gary Cooper and Ingrid Bergman, the film had had a War Bond premiere in Washington attended by scores of celebrities and government notables like Admiral King and Harry Hopkins. Five million people had already read Ernest Hemingway's bestseller.

The Organization of Colored Locomotive Firemen was again threatening to march on Washington to compel President Roosevelt to abolish 'Jim Crowism'. I wanted the march to go forward. I didn't think colored people would ever get free of discrimination unless they held more marches and sit-ins. Joe sided with most of the rest of the country who said that during the war race conflicts would hurt the war effort. Of course, Joe was a man. I had a different perspective. If women were being encouraged to return to domesticity after the war, then the Negro would be pressured to take up his past role too. The government needed us now. They had to pay attention to us. Would they after the war?

After Joe paid the check he helped me out of my seat. 'Let's go catch a bus,' he said. 'I'll show you my new place.'

I could feel Joe's breath and his soft beard on my neck and the warmth of the length of his naked body pressed up to mine. We were spooned into one of the two single beds in the only bedroom in Joe and Ken's tiny apartment. Without a word we'd gone straight to the bedroom after we'd arrived, pausing only long enough to lower the window blinds.

'I've got to get up,' I said to Joe.

'No, not yet,' he said. 'Stay.'

'Can't. Must go!'

He sighed and unwrapped his arms from around my body. I slipped out of the bed and hurried to the bathroom. When I returned to the bedroom he was gone, leaving behind the depression in the bed where we'd loved each other. I got dressed quickly and went through the living room and into the tiny kitchenette, where I found Joe making a pot of coffee. I slipped under his arm and we kissed.

'Do you know it's four o'clock in the afternoon?' he said.

'We must have fallen asleep,' I answered.

'How long can you stay?'

'I should leave soon. I told Phoebe I was having lunch with

a friend and going shopping. She'll expect me back in time for dinner.'

Joe and I never discussed regularizing our relationship. He would always be a foreign refugee. The JDC, his employer, had become a clandestine organization the minute Germany had declared war on us, so his work was illegal. Even if we married I might lose my job. Besides, I didn't know much about him, just what he told me, and I wasn't convinced some of it wasn't a cover story. All that stuff about his Czech grand-parents and their dairy farm and their Holstein-Friesen cows and milkmaids! I was only sure that he was a Czech national who went to university in England. He had a British passport. I knew that he worked for the JDC because I saw him at his office. His cover story while he lived at 'Two Trees' was that he was a Slavic language instructor at George Washington University. I was also positive that Joe was one of the good guys, whatever secrets he might be keeping from me.

As for Joe's intentions, he simply told me he wasn't free to marry. Which was fine with me. I wasn't in a rush to remarry. I liked earning my own money and doing what I pleased. If my parents even suspected I thought this way it would shock them to their core. And that would be before they found out I hadn't been to church a single Sunday since I'd arrived in Washington.

I curled up on the corduroy sofa in the small living room. Joe brought me my cup of coffee and settled down next to me. The apartment was tiny, a typical two and a half, with a living room, a bedroom with twin beds, a bathroom and a kitchenette. Rent would be about ninety dollars a month. Hundreds of similar apartments had been renovated and built to accommodate the flood of war workers that flooded Washington. Joe and Ken's place was in a large complex called Potomac Plaza two blocks west of George Washington University in Foggy Bottom, about five long blocks from my boarding house. The building itself couldn't be less impressive despite its size, but the apartment was cozy, and I liked the anonymity of it. It would make a great safe house, if I was in the business of looking for one.

Joe got up to answer the telephone in the bedroom and I allowed my mind to review the story of the two prisoners of war who'd died, or committed suicide, crossing the Atlantic. Ever since I'd learned they lived at the same address in the Sudetenland, been conscripted on the same day and vanished on the same day months later, I'd been obsessed with their perplexing story. I gathered from Miss Osborne's comments that she felt the same. But the camp commander and the captain of the ship were sure the two men had killed themselves, so there wasn't much we could do about it. Solving their murders wasn't part of our mission. Our job was to identify prisoners we could recruit to go behind German lines in Italy with new identities and distribute black propaganda. Period. But if a killer lurked in the prisoner-of-war camp, and the prisoners knew it, couldn't this obstruct our mission? Who would volunteer to help us if there was a murderer in the camp? I had selfish reasons for worrying about this too. I wanted my first assignment for my new job to be a success.

'You look like you're miles away from here,' Joe said, slipping back on to the sofa and putting his arm around me again. 'What are you daydreaming about?'

'I am so sorry,' I said. 'My mind wandered off for a minute.'

'I must be forgettable,' he said, smiling.

'You know that's not true!' I said, upset with myself.

'I'm just teasing you,' he said, pulling me closer to him. 'God knows there's plenty to think about. I suppose your new job?'

Without hesitation I acted on my plan to ask Joe to help me, without Miss Osborne's approval.

'I have a question for you,' I said. 'About an incident that we're investigating at work.'

'If I can help I'd be glad to.'

'Two ethnic German men lived in Reichenberg, in the Sudetenland, at the same address. They were drafted into the Wehrmacht on the same day, but into different units. Both men served in North Africa and were captured by Allied forces. They were sent here to a prisoner-of-war camp, but before they arrived they both vanished off the Liberty Ship ferrying them to the states. They died on the same day. Where else could they go but overboard, of course, and the naval authorities ruled that they had both committed suicide.'

Joe arched an eyebrow. 'Really?' he said. 'That's odd. So with all those coincidences, you're wondering if there was another reason they vanished.'

'Yes,' I said, taking the final swallow of my coffee. 'Do you think it's reasonable to wonder if they were murdered?'

Joe finished his own coffee and set the cup on to the packing crate that served as a cocktail table. 'Yes,' he said, 'I think it is perfectly reasonable. I mean, the coincidences aren't that striking until the two men disappear together. They were out of the war for the duration; why should they want to kill themselves? And on the same day too?'

'That's what bothers me. But if they were murdered, who did it, and why?'

'If they were assigned to different units then they didn't spend any time together during the war?'

'Apparently not.'

'OK.' Joe sat in thought for a few minutes. 'They lived at the same address, were drafted on the same day, and when they were brought back together as prisoners of war, they both died on the same day. Or were murdered.'

'Yes.'

'They must have seen something before they were drafted. Or learned something. About a German, or Germans, I would assume; only the Germans would have the authority to conscript them. What they knew caught up with them on that ship.'

Joe's conclusion agreed with my own. If the two men were murdered it had to be that their deaths were related to their lives while they lived in Reichenberg, before they went into the Wehrmacht.

I gripped Joe's arm. 'Thank you,' I said. 'That was a great help. Do you know anything about Reichenberg?'

Joe shrugged. 'Not really. Been through it a few times on the train, well before the war. Of course everything there is different now.' Now that the Sudetenland was part of the German Reich. 'Do you know where those two men lived?' Joe asked. 'I can ask my Czech colleagues at work if they're familiar with the neighborhood.'

I should have hesitated, but I didn't. I gave him the address.

'I'll see what I can find out,' he said.

I didn't let Joe walk me to my bus stop. Now that I had a better job I felt even more vulnerable being with him than I had in the past. His accent, charming as it was to me, just attracted too much attention.

Agent Gray Williams was waiting for me at the bus stop. I'd wondered if he knew about Joe, and now I had my answer. I suppressed the urge to walk away. I knew there was no point. He knew where to find me.

I sat down next to him. 'What do you want?' I asked.

Williams put down the newspaper he'd been pretending to read. 'Why, Mrs Pearlie,' he said. 'What a coincidence.'

'How did you know I was here?'

'Just a guess. I knew Mr Prager was back in town, and since you're such great friends, I thought you might show up for a visit.' I shouldn't have been surprised that Williams knew Joe. The FBI kept a close watch on the JDC, since it was staffed with Jews, refugees and socialists, all special obsessions of Director Hoover. The FBI files rivaled ours at OSS in their size and completeness.

'How did you know where Joe lived?'

Williams waited until a woman with a wailing baby in a pram passed us by.

'We had him followed, what do you think? He works for a covert organization.'

'A charity that smuggles Jewish refugees out of Europe. How subversive.'

'He's a Czech. The country is a part of Germany now.'

'Joe has a British passport. Last I heard Britain was our ally,' I said.

'He was born a Czech. If he's not a Nazi sympathizer he's probably a Communist.'

'He's not. But I would be if my country had been invaded by Hitler and no one in the world had lifted a finger to help.'

'You just don't know all the facts, Mrs Pearlie,' Williams said, in a tone of voice suitable for a recalcitrant child.

I was furious. I had worked for months now for America's spy agency. I had Top Secret clearance. I knew plenty of facts, and would have liked nothing better than to tell him so. But I had to control my temper and keep my mouth shut. Not just because it was my job, but because I didn't want to anger him. He knew too much about me, and about Joe, and his waiting here at the bus stop for me was proof.

'My bus will be here soon,' I said. 'So I'll ask you again, what is it you want from me?'

'What I told you at Fort Meade. Information. The FBI is responsible for domestic security and counterespionage inside the United States. Not the OSS. I expect you to deliver to me every scrap of information you and your colleagues collect from the prisoners you interview at Fort Meade.'

'No,' I said.

'You have no choice.'

'You can get access to the information you need through regular channels,' I said, as calmly as if we were discussing the last Senators baseball game. 'Speak to Miss Osborne, she's in charge of the operation. Of course, you could always make use of the FBI agents that have infiltrated OSS.'

That hit home. I could see Agent Williams' expression change from cocky to concerned.

'Director Donovan knows who they are,' I added. 'Every last one of them.'

I could see my bus coming and stood up.

Williams jumped up next to me and grabbed my arm to restrain me. 'We're not done talking,' he said. 'Don't get on that bus. You're not Diana Prince, you know.'

I pulled my arm out of his grasp. That was the last straw. Diana Prince was a comic book character, a clerk who worked in an intelligence agency and fought the Nazis as her alter ego, Wonder Woman. She was the secretary – what else? – to the Justice Society of America. I'd read one issue of the comic, and it seemed to me that Wonder Woman spent most of her time mooning over Steve Trevor.

Williams' remark was unforgivable. I was finished being afraid of what he could do to my career. I'd already told Miss Osborne about him, and I felt sure she would back me up if he tried to blackmail me.

'I'm not your snitch,' I said to him. The bus stopped, its door clanged open and I climbed on board, leaving Williams standing on the sidewalk.

NINE

Inside the German mess most of the tables and chairs had been shoved up against the canvas walls of the tent. The remaining table stood in the middle of the room with twenty chairs arranged in short rows in front of it. A large cross, roughly fashioned from scrap timber, stood in the center of the table. Next to it was a man wearing khaki with 'PW' stenciled on the back of his shirt and a Bible tucked under his arm. An ugly red scar ranged down the left side of his face. A nasty black eye had faded to purple and yellow. His congregation, what there was of it, also consisted of prisoners of war.

'We only have a few hymnals and prayer books,' Lt Bahnsen, the scarred man, said. 'We'll just do our best. Let's start by singing "Jesus Sinners Doth Receive". Most of us know that one, don't we?' The congregation and its leader began to sing enthusiastically and badly.

Outside the tent two army MPs guarded the entrance to the makeshift church. A war dog slept at their feet.

'I don't like it,' Corporal Steesen said. 'Why do they have their own Sunday service? What's wrong with the one the camp provides?'

'They want to pray in German,' said his colleague, Private Jenkins.

'That don't mean we have to let them do it.'

'I think we do. It's in the Geneva Convention.'

'Damn the Geneva Convention! You don't think the Nazis care about the Geneva Convention, do you?'

Inside the tent Lt Bahnsen held up a hand. 'If we say we have no sin we deceive ourselves, and the truth is not in us.'

His congregation answered, 'But if we confess our sins God, who is faithful and just, will forgive our sins and cleanse us from all unrighteousness.'

And Bahnsen answered, 'Let us then confess our sins to God our Father.'

'Even the damn dog is bored,' Steesen said, nudging the animal with his foot. He rested his rifle against his leg and pulled out a package of cigarettes and a box of matches.

'What are you doing?' Jenkins said. 'We're on guard duty!'

'I don't care,' Steesen said. 'If I have to listen to all that German singing going on the least I deserve is a cigarette. Besides, do you see anybody? It's Sunday. The officers are all off paying golf or taking their wives to lunch at the officers' club.'

Jenkins cocked an ear. 'That sounds like the Lord's Prayer,' he said.

'You don't know what it is,' Steesen said. 'It could be the Nazi creed, or the devil's pledge.'

'I don't think so. It's got the right rhythm. I'm sure it's the Lord's Prayer.'

'Oh, shut up,' Steesen said. 'Do you think our boys in German POW camps are attending their own church services now? Do you think they're getting ham and apple pie for Sunday dinner? Do you think the Nazis are following the bloody Geneva Convention? Treating these guys like our own brothers is the sin happening here.'

'Shut up yourself,' Jenkins said. 'If you don't like it fill out a complaint slip and take it to the chaplain.'

Inside Bahnsen's congregation rose to its feet. 'Turn in your hymnal to "The Son of God Goes Forth to War",' he said. 'And be reminded that there is more than one kind of war.'

After the service Hans Marek stayed behind to help Lt Bahnsen clean up and set up the mess hall again. When they were done reordering the tables and chairs Marek touched Lt Bahnsen's arm. 'Father,' he began, in his halting German.

'Hans, I am not a priest,' Bahnsen said. 'Call me Lt Bahnsen, please.'

'But you're almost a priest.'

'Almost doesn't count in this business,' Bahnsen said, smiling.

Marek kept his grip on Bahnsen's sleeve. 'But I want to make confession,' he said.

If Bahnsen's face hadn't been so sore he would have raised both eyebrows. 'Hans, I just reminded you that I'm not a priest. I can't provide absolution. The General Confession in the service will have to do.'

'Please,' Marek said. 'It's important to me. I need to talk to you. I don't care if you can't absolve me. I just need you to listen to me. You can't tell anyone what I say, can you?'

'I wouldn't do that,' Bahnsen said. 'But all right, if you understand my limits, let's find two chairs and we can talk about what's bothering you.'

A German prisoner of war, one of the SS riflemen, passed by the open flap of a window into the mess tent just in time to see Marek kneeling at Bahnsen's feet, talking.

My valise was looking mighty small but it was all the luggage I could take, no matter how many weeks we'd need to stay at Fort Meade. I'd need to carry the case full of documents and my handbag too, and whether we flew or not luggage space was limited. Even if we had Private McVey or another soldier assigned to us it was important to me that I be able to carry my own things if necessary.

I'd told Phoebe I'd be out of town for a week again, but the truth was if we worked on Saturdays I could be at Fort Meade for several weeks. We had most of the prisoners of war left to interview. The weather was cooling off too. I decided to wear my fur-collared coat and my lightweight wool army green shirtwaist to travel in. I'd pack a menswear grey wool suit, collarless and bound in green, that I'd just bought at Woodies, black corduroy trousers, a green cardigan that I could wear with the suit skirt and the trousers and a couple of white blouses. I wrapped my pearls and a pair of earrings in my pajamas. After I tucked in some underwear, which I could wash out in the bathroom, I was relieved to see that I still had room for the new pint bottle of Gordon's gin I'd bought on the way home from Joe's yesterday, a nip of vermouth and a can of cashews. And a tin cup for cocktails in our billet, of course.

*　　*　　*

Hanzi tired of waiting for reveille. His bladder was full; surely the guards would let him use the latrine. He rolled over on his cot, but his face encountered something on his pillow that didn't belong there. Things, rather, that rustled when his cheek touched them. He recoiled, and as his eyes adjusted he saw the pile of gnawed chicken bones arranged on his pillow. Hanzi screamed, startling his tent-mates awake. One of them turned on a light, and in its glow Hanzi saw that the bones weren't just stripped clean of meat, they were charred too. Terrified, he cowered on his cot with his blanket wrapped around him, trembling, almost blinded by flashing spots of terror exploding in his field of vision. When his tent-mates saw the bones they fled the tent, calling out for help.

The next thing Hanzi knew Lt Bahnsen was urging him off his cot and outside. An MP stood with a war dog on his leash behind him, the dog barking and straining on his harness. Bahnsen half dragged Hanzi out of the tent, but the dog kept barking and growling at the pile of bones.

Outside a crowd of prisoners gathered. Hanzi had stopped screaming, but still trembled with shock as Bahnsen kept an arm around his shoulders and spoke to him gently.

Kapp stood over the two men. 'What has happened here?' he asked.

'When Private Hanzi awoke he found charred chicken bones in his cot,' Bahnsen said. 'You wouldn't know anything about that, would you?'

'Not at all,' Kapp said. 'Why would I?'

Bahnsen urged Hanzi to his feet. 'You,' he said to Hanzi's roommates, 'leave the bones as they are for now. The Americans will want to see them. Collect some clothes for Private Hanzi and bring them to my tent. He can change there.'

'I believe it's my job to give the orders here,' Kapp said.

'Of course,' Bahnsen said. 'Do you have anything to add, Major?'

'No. But *I* will inform Lt Rawlins of what has happened, not you.'

'Yes, sir,' Bahnsen answered. 'Come on,' he said to Hanzi,

'by the time we've changed hot coffee will be ready in the mess. You'll feel better after a cup.'

We headed back to Fort Meade by air again. I recognized our plane as the same one we took last week, the one that was identical to the Lockheed Electra 10 Amelia Earhart was flying when she disappeared. But, gee whiz, she was lost over the vast Pacific Ocean. If we crashed our wreckage would be easy to find in the Maryland countryside.

I came prepared. My large handbag contained my own paper bags in case I got sick and an apple if I missed a meal.

True to her word Miss Osborne brought me a case for the prisoner-of-war documents we'd prepared. The canvas olive drab messenger bag had more than enough pockets, buckles and straps to make anyone carrying it feel official. The young seaman loading our luggage into the underbelly of the airplane wanted me to store the case there, but I insisted on taking it into the airplane with me.

Merle and I followed Miss Osborne up the ladder into the passenger compartment and squeezed our way down the aisle. I wasn't the only person on the flight who'd brought extra cases on board. An army colonel had an attaché case hand-cuffed to his wrist. Another officer kept what I recognized as a suitcase radio between his legs in front of him. I wondered where he and the radio were headed.

We landed without incident and were met by Private McVey driving an army staff car. It was a two-door Ford sedan without insignia or flags flying. Two of us had to climb into a narrow back seat, but it was more comfortable than a jeep.

'Where to first, ma'am?' McVey asked Miss Osborne.

'We need to drop off our bags, then go straight to the stockade,' she answered.

'Welcome back,' Rawlins said, extending his right hand to each of us, holding a steaming cup of coffee in the other. He must have noticed our eyes fixed on it. 'Coffee?' he asked. We'd only had time for one cup before we headed for the airport and we eagerly accepted.

'There's a fresh pot in my office,' Rawlins said.

We crowded around the coffee pot, staying hot on an electric ring on top of a file cabinet, and dosed our java with cream and sugar. I was the only person who noticed Rawlins slipping a half-empty pint of Old Forester bourbon sitting on his desk into a drawer. His eyes met mine, and he shrugged.

It was none of my business if the man spiked his morning coffee. I remembered what Miss Osborne had told me, that prisoner-of-war camp officers tended to be unfit for combat duty for some reason. Perhaps drinking was Lt Rawlins' weakness. As long as he could do his job, at least regarding our mission, I didn't care.

Rawlins cleared his throat, and Merle, Miss Osborne and I turned to him.

'We've had some trouble here,' Rawlins said. 'It involves one of the men you interviewed while you were here last week. You know we located Hans Marek in Baltimore. He's back in camp, in his billet.'

'That's all?' Merle said. 'He's not been punished?'

'Under the Geneva Convention he's permitted to escape,' Rawlins said. 'In fact it's the duty of all captured soldiers, including ours, to escape if they can. Now if he committed a felony, or damaged property, we could arrest him. But he didn't. We've added a guard with a war dog at the base of all the watchtowers at night to keep prisoners from climbing up the supports again.'

'You mentioned an incident involving one of the men?' I asked.

'Yes,' Rawlins said. 'When Thomas Hanzi woke up this morning he rolled over into a pile of gnawed chicken bones. The bones were stacked like wood for a fire, and most were charred.'

'My God,' I said. 'How awful.'

'How did he react?' Miss Osborne asked. 'Is he OK?'

'He was terrified, of course. Screaming. He almost lost consciousness. Lt Bahnsen got him out of the tent and calmed him down.'

'Do you have any idea who might have done this?' I asked.

'None,' Rawlins said. 'But he is, as you know, a gypsy.'

I saw Miss Osborne's jaw muscles clench. 'So you think he was being persecuted by the Nazis in the camp. Kapp and who else?'

'Lt Steiner is Waffen SS. So are two ordinary soldiers, just privates, who are SS riflemen. They would obey any order from Kapp or Steiner instantly. Regular soldiers in the Wehrmacht, like most of the POWs, aren't permitted to join political parties, but of course many are just as loyal to the Nazi Party as the four Waffen SS men.'

'You've got to protect him,' Miss Osborne said. 'He's terribly vulnerable.'

'There's not much we can do. We did move Hanzi into Lt Bahnsen's tent because Bahnsen consoled him after the incident. He seems to have taken on that role in the camp. And we have notified the Swiss Legation and the Red Cross. They'll investigate the incident. Maybe some of the prisoners will talk to them.'

I didn't think that would be enough. OSS had done a number of psychological studies on the Nazis. They tended to be without empathy, and enjoyed exercising power over people just for the sake of it. In a prisoner-of-war camp there wouldn't be much for this kind of person to do except harass vulnerable prisoners.

'Now, you asked to speak to Jens Geller first this morning, correct?' Rawlins said. 'He's waiting for you at the interview tent.'

'Thank you,' Miss Osborne said.

'This incident involving Thomas Hanzi is bad news for us,' Miss Osborne said, as we waited for a military policeman to bring Geller into the interview tent. 'If there's a hardline Nazi faction in this camp, one committed enough to torment Hanzi because he's a gypsy, it will be difficult for us to recruit any of the prisoners to volunteer for our mission, no matter how the interviews go. They'll be too afraid.'

'Can't we get rid of Major Kapp somehow?' I asked. 'He must be the ringleader.'

'There's talk of a special prisoner-of-war camp just for officers, but it's months away from being completed,' she said. 'We need volunteers to penetrate the Nazi lines in northern Italy now.'

MP Steesen, who appeared to be permanently attached to us, escorted Jens Geller into the tent.

'Be careful what you say,' Miss Osborne said softly. 'The camp authorities thought only Kapp knew English, but it turned out Bahnsen did too. And Geller reacted to a slur in English from a guard. Starting now we won't speak freely to each other during interviews until we know for certain the prisoner doesn't understand us.'

Steesen shoved Geller into the chair at the table in front of us. Like most of the prisoners, Geller was thin and maintained his soldier's posture, sitting almost at attention in his chair. He still wore his hair in the German fashion, like Hitler, oiled and parted on the side with his bangs slicked down toward one eyebrow. As he fiddled with a box of matches I noticed that the tips of his fingers were stained brown.

Miss Osborne clicked on the recording machine to begin the interview. Geller glanced at it with curiosity as the tapes began to circle.

'Mr Geller,' Miss Osborne began.

'Unteroffizier Geller,' he answered.

'Sergeant Geller,' she continued. 'I understand that you were a motorcycle messenger for the Three Hundred Thirty-fourth Infantry of the Afrika Korps, that you were captured at Bizerte.' Merle translated.

At hearing Merle's voice Geller broke into a huge smile. 'Texas,' he said in English to Merle. 'Cowboy?'

Merle played along with him. 'Sure,' he said. 'I'm from Amarillo.'

'John Wayne,' Geller said.

This time it was Merle's turn to laugh. 'Not exactly,' he said. 'How much English can you speak?'

Geller shrugged. 'Movies only English,' he said. '*Stagecoach. Destry Rides Again.*'

'Where did you live that you could see American movies?' Miss Osborne asked.

Geller looked at Merle quizzically, and he translated into German.

'Berlin,' Geller said. 'My father was a shopkeeper, a tobacconist. We rolled our own cigarettes.' Which was why his fingers were stained, I thought. 'He gave me just enough money every Saturday afternoon so I could see a movie. Even after I finished my schooling, room and board and a movie was all he could pay me.'

'I see from your papers that you enlisted,' Miss Osborne said.

'I was eager to be a Reich soldier,' Geller said. 'Fighting for the eternal Fatherland has a such a nice ring to it, don't you think?'

I heard the sarcasm in Geller's voice even before Merle translated his words.

'You are loyal to the Reich, then,' Miss Osborne said.

'In the beginning,' he answered, 'it was all so glorious. Especially to a young man who had endured years of humiliation and poverty. Who could only look forward to selling cigarettes and pipe tobacco for just enough money for his family to live, barely live. Once the Nazis gained power, red banners flew on every building, huge swastikas many stories high hung from the Reichstag, enormous cheering crowds filled the Königsplatz, thousands of soldiers goose-stepped in front of the Reichstag, their hands raised toward the Führer on his viewing platform. It was better than any American movie. Who didn't want to be a part of it all? Within months all European German-speaking people were united under the Reich. Then we conquered France and had our revenge for the Versailles Treaty. Even *Kristallnacht* didn't dissuade us from our path.'

Still the sarcasm leaked through Geller's German.

'Except that Germany hasn't won the war,' Miss Osborne said quietly.

Geller stared at her for so long we thought he might not speak again. He looked around the room, as if he expected someone to be eavesdropping. Then he nodded at the tape recorder. Miss Osborne reached over to the machine and shut it off. The rotating tapes slowed to a stop. Geller leaned back in his chair and lit a cigarette from a pack of Camels stuck into his shirt pocket.

'Germany will not win the war,' Geller said at last, translated by Merle. 'That wanker Hitler invaded Russia. Russia! He thought he could succeed where Napoleon failed! Pfft! No army in the world can conquer Russia. Stalin will throw millions of men at us, and the Americans and British will invade from the west, and the only question is who will get to Berlin first, and how many Germans will die.'

I wrote on my steno pad, in capital letters, 'I THINK THIS MAN IS OURS.'

'I gather you would like the war to end soon,' Miss Osborne said.

Geller leaned over the table. 'I have two younger brothers in the Wehrmacht. What do you think? I don't want them to die for nothing.'

'You could help us shorten the war, you know. By working with us. The sooner Germany surrenders the more likely that your brothers will survive,' Miss Osborne said.

Geller stared at the floor while finishing his cigarette.

'I don't know,' he said.

'What is holding you back?'

'I don't want to die.'

'Of course not,' Miss Osborne said.

'I'm not safe now,' he said. 'You heard what happened to the gypsy, Hanzi? If a word, even a word, of collaboration between a prisoner and American intelligence gets out!' Geller drew his finger across his throat.

I wondered what Miss Osborne would say to that.

'We are recruiting for a top-secret operation,' Miss Osborne said. 'It will be dangerous. But you would have the same training, and protection, as our own agents.'

Geller crushed his cigarette into an ashtray, then immediately lit another one.

'I will think about it,' he said. 'But I'd like to go now, please. I've already said too much.'

'In a minute. Sergeant Geller, did you know the men who died on the voyage across the Atlantic?'

'You mean the soldiers who killed themselves?' he asked. He shook his head. 'No. You remember the Germans were split between holds. They were in Hold Two. I was in Hold Five with that pig-dog, Steiner.'

Miss Osborne nodded at Steesen to take Geller back to the stockade.

Before he left, though, Geller pointed at Merle's boots. 'Cowboy boots,' he said. 'How much?'

'Seven bucks,' Merle answered, grinning.

Geller threw his hands in the air. 'I do not have!' he said, also smiling.

'Maybe after the war,' Merle said.

'I will remember that,' Geller said on his way out of the tent.

'If we bribed Geller with your boots, Merle, maybe we could turn him,' I said, passing him sour cream to heap on his chili.

'It would be a sacrifice on my part,' Merle said, 'but for a good cause.'

'We can do better than that,' Miss Osborne said. 'I expect we could come up with a brand new pair of cowboy boots for Sergeant Geller.'

'I think there's a western outfitter on the Virginia side of the Potomac,' I said, enjoying my chili too. It had at least as much meat as beans in it.

'All joking aside, I think he's a good prospect. What do you think, Louise?'

'I agree. I mean, the man basically admitted that he was a Nazi supporter until Hitler invaded Russia, and now he thinks Germany will lose the war. And he's got two brothers in the Wehrmacht. The sooner the war ends the better their chances of survival.'

'As long as there's an SS Major in charge of this camp I worry no one will cooperate with us,' Miss Osborne said. 'Geller did say his personal safety had to be guaranteed. I can hardly blame him.'

'You said we could protect him,' I said to her.

'I exaggerated. Right now we don't know what we're going to do with the prisoners we recruit; we don't have safe houses prepared or training organized yet. Washington is working on it.'

'Can't we isolate our recruits in the camp, if we get any, once they've been selected?' Merle said.

'Kapp and his minions – because he's bound to have minions – will know at once if they're isolated or sent to another location. And all these men have families back in Germany and many have relatives in the Wehrmacht,' she said. 'The prisoners will be worried about their safety.'

'Thanks to the Red Cross all the prisoners, including Kapp, can write letters home. Some of them could be coded,' I said. I'd already had direct experience with a coded postcard. Its innocent message had signaled a major operation that we at OSS almost missed.

'Kapp won't need to write coded letters,' Miss Osborne said, buttering a piece of cornbread, 'not when he can punish anyone he wants right here in the camp. What was to stop our gypsy friend Hanzi from being murdered last night? Nothing.'

Chantal, the Red Cross representative, slipped into a chair at our table while we were finishing our coffee. 'Have you heard?' he asked. Then, 'What is that?' when he spotted Merle's chili.

'It's chili,' Merle said. 'Want to try some?'

'*Mon Dieu*, no! It smells like charcoal. And are those red beans? Horrible things!'

'Enough about the chili,' Miss Osborne said. 'What did you want to tell us, Lucien?'

'Hans Marek's escaped again,' he said.

'In broad daylight?' I said. 'How?'

'In the kitchen garbage,' Chantal said. 'No one searched it before it was trucked to the dump.'

I knew an FBI agent who would be furious. Clearly Marek wasn't the saboteur type, he just wanted to have some fun, but Agent Williams would take any escape as a black mark on his record.

'Marek must have sold more of those ribbons and badges,' Merle said, 'so he has money to spend on girls.'

'I'm sure the FBI has all the usual places staked out,' Miss Osborne said. 'Have you been able to find out anything about Aach and Muntz, the men who supposedly killed themselves on the crossing?'

'Nothing much that we didn't already know,' Chantal said. 'They lived at the same address in Reichenberg. They were conscripted on the same day, which is not unlikely, considering how methodically the Germans do business. According to the other prisoners on the ship they spent a lot of time together. All that is within the realm of possibility.'

'Dying, or killing themselves, on the same day isn't,' Miss Osborne said.

Chantal threw his hands in the air. 'There were no witnesses, at least none that will admit it. The men just vanished off the deck during their exercise time.'

'The truth is no one cares how they died,' Miss Osborne said. 'Except us.

And what about the incident this morning, the burnt chicken bones that Thomas Hanzi found in his bunk?'

'The tents aren't secured,' Chantal said. 'Anyone could have sneaked in between guard patrols during the night and constructed that little charnel house. That poor young man was terrified. Lt Bahnsen was quite kind to him, though. I believe Bahnsen was studying for the Lutheran priesthood before the war? Did you know he holds a prayer service on Sundays in the mess tent?'

'Does anyone go?'

'A few.'

I reminded myself to change my assessment of Marek in my notebook. He was too impulsive for an undercover mission. So far, of all the prisoners we'd interviewed, I'd only starred Bahnsen and Geller. OSS would need dozens. Of course many more POWs would arrive in the States, but timeliness was so important. Back in Washington and in our London office propaganda materials were already being designed and constructed, as well as authentic uniforms and forged identity papers. We needed reliable native German speakers to deliver them safely behind German lines.

I wondered how many more prisoners we could recruit if SS Major Kapp wasn't the senior German in the camp. And if two prisoners of war hadn't died mysteriously on the way to the States. And if someone hadn't threatened Thomas Hanzi with a pyre built of chicken bones on his bed.

That afternoon we interviewed four more German prisoners of war. One was seventeen years old. He'd been conscripted right out of military school and sent straight to Tunisia to load flak anti-aircraft guns. 'Way too young,' I wrote in my notes. Another German's hands shook so much he couldn't light his own cigarette; Merle had to strike his match and hold his hand steady for him. His voice trembled when he spoke. We could hear the fear in his voice even without translation. 'Terrible case of nerves,' I wrote in my notebook.

The last two prisoners we spoke with were laborers with little education. 'Not trainable,' I wrote.

The three of us stayed in the interview room to read through and discuss my notes.

Miss Osborne shut my notebook and handed it back to me. 'I agree with you, Louise,' she said. 'I think Bahnsen and Geller are our only possibilities so far, and I'm not so sure about Bahnsen.'

'The man was drafted out of seminary,' I said. 'How could he not be willing to help us beat the Nazis?'

'I have a odd feeling about him,' Miss Osborne said. 'He seemed to have made his own plans, and wasn't sure they would fit into ours. It was nothing he said. Just intuition.'

I dreaded eating dinner in the prisoners' mess again, but Miss Osborne said it was a good way to observe the prisoners outside the interview room. As always the food was plentiful and full of rationed goodies: roast pork, fresh butter and rich desserts.

Major Lucas was AWOL again tonight, enjoying his meal at the Fort Meade officers' mess, where he didn't have to watch German prisoners of war stuffing themselves with the same food he and his soldiers were eating.

So there were just five of us of us at the head table in the POW mess tonight, Lt Rawlins, Mr Chantal and the three of us from OSS. Agent Williams was missing too, out in hot pursuit of Hans Marek, I assumed.

I'd just started spooning up my chocolate pudding when Steiner, the Nazi SS officer we'd interviewed earlier, erupted from his seat and began to scream and point at Thomas Hanzi, who startled at the shouting and quailed back into his chair. Steiner picked up a heavy water pitcher and flung it at him, just missing his head. Kapp jumped to his feet, overturning his chair, and clenched his fists, his jaw muscles pulsing in his face. The rest of the Germans at the table retreated, upsetting dishes and throwing chairs out of the way as they fled.

The MPs guarding us unholstered their side arms and looked to Rawlins for orders. Rawlins shook his head at them.

'Aren't you going to do anything?' Chantal asked Lt Rawlins. Rawlins shook his head again. 'Let Kapp handle it, unless there's real violence – he's in command.'

Steiner pointed at Hanzi while shouting with Kapp, and whatever he said enraged the major. Kapp picked up the water pitcher Steiner had thrown, smashed it on the edge of the table, shattering it into pieces, and advanced on Steiner, gripping the pitcher handle still attached to a jagged chunk of glass.

Chantal jumped to his feet. 'This looks like violence to me,' he said to Rawlins.

'I'm in charge here,' Rawlins said. 'Sit down.' Chantal did as he was told, but he was clearly upset. I gripped Miss Osborne's hand, and she squeezed back. 'It's OK,' she whispered to me. 'Smart of Rawlins to let them fight it out.'

Kapp and Steiner glared at each other across the table, breathing hard. The other prisoners collected at the back of the room. They were silent, but closely watched the showdown between the two SS officers. I could see they were nervous about the outcome, and I wondered which of the men they wanted to prevail. Bahnsen was still seated at his table, one arm draped across his chair back. Unlike most of the other prisoners he didn't look frightened, only bemused. Hanzi stood right behind him, as if for protection.

Steiner leaned on the table and placed a hand flat on the tablecloth. He said something roughly in German, clearly questioning Kapp's authority. Before anyone could intervene Kapp charged Steiner and rammed the jagged edge of the broken pitcher he still held deep into Steiner's hand. Blood spurted out of the injury all over the white tablecloth. Steiner screamed, clutching his wounded hand to his chest. Kapp said something to him in a calm but threatening voice.

Rawlins finally decided it was time to intervene. He ordered two MPs to seize Steiner and take him to the medical officer and then to solitary confinement. On his way out of the tent, blood dripping from his napkin-wrapped hand, Steiner threw a phrase back at Kapp I actually understood. '*Geh zum Teufel!*' Go to hell! Once Steiner was out of the room Kapp beckoned to the German prisoners, ordering them back to their tables. They came quietly, slipping into their seats to finish their meal. Kapp's table finished eating amid shards of broken glass scattered across the blood-stained tablecloth.

After the Germans finished dinner and marched out of the mess tent the five of us who'd eaten at the head table poured coffee for ourselves and discussed the incident.

'Do you know what they said to each other?' I asked Merle.

'I have no idea,' he said. 'I didn't recognize most of the words. Except at the end, when Kapp stabbed Steiner, he said, "Not him," referring to Hanzi, I think. That's all I got.'

'Mr Chantal, could you understand anything they said?' Lt Rawlins asked the Red Cross representative.

'It was so confused and noisy, but Kapp called Steiner *ein Drecksack*, a dirty bastard, before Kapp stabbed him with the broken water pitcher.'

'Do you know what Steiner was saying when he was screaming at Hanzi?' Miss Osborne asked.

Chantal stirred his coffee cup in silence.

'Well, Mr Chantal?' Lt Rawlins asked.

Chantal looked at Miss Osborne and me, and then back to

Rawlins. 'I'm not comfortable with ladies present. Perhaps Miss Osborne and Mrs Pearlie could leave us for a minute?'

'Don't be absurd,' Miss Osborne said. 'Spit it out!'

'I insist you tell us, Mr Chantal, what Steiner shouted at Hanzi,' Lt Rawlins said.

'Steiner called Hanzi *ein Stricher*. A rent boy.'

Chantal's bombshell met with shocked silence. Miss Osborne broke it. 'Well then, that would cause a commotion,' she said. 'Lt Rawlins,' she continued, 'I urge you to provide Mr Hanzi with special protection. He's got gypsy blood, first of all. He's been cruelly harassed. And Steiner, at least, believes he's a homosexual. He's practically got a target painted on his back for the Nazis to aim at.'

'I don't think that's necessary, Miss Osborne. Major Kapp defused the situation. He understands his men and how to handle them better than we do. He's as hardline as possible, he's SS, and still he protected Hanzi. But I will order the guards to keep a close watch on Steiner.'

Rawlins loosened his tie and unfastened the top button of his shirt. He looked worn out.

'I need a drink. You're all welcome to join me at the officers' club.'

'Does the club have a radio?' Miss Osborne asked.

'Sure,' Lt Rawlins said. 'And there's always a game of bridge or poker going on.'

TEN

Miss Osborne and I went back to our quarters just long enough to change clothes and freshen up. Since we'd been sitting all day we decided to walk to the officers' club. I wore my trousers and sweater and was thankful for them. The air had a definite chill to it, and the sidewalks were strewn with fallen flame-colored leaves. Millions of stars shone brightly in the clear, crowded night sky. Somewhere on the base a military band was playing a lively tune but the sound was too soft for me to identify the music.

Miss Osborne walked beside me with her hands stuffed into her pants pockets. 'This time next year we might be in Europe,' she said.

'Good God,' I said. 'Is that all the time we have to get ready? A year!'

'Yes, and I don't know how President Roosevelt gets through his day,' Miss Osborne said. 'He must be under enormous pressure.'

'He has Harry Hopkins,' I said.

'Who is missing half his stomach.'

'And General Eisenhower. And the British.'

'Thank God for the British,' Miss Osborne said. 'To think we almost abandoned them.'

The club, which included nurses, since they were officers too, was jury-rigged in a Quonset hut just outside the stockade entrance. Merle was already inside, seated at a poker game with his cards in one hand and a beer in the other. A vicious game of darts went on in another corner. Miss Osborne broke her own rule of not drinking in public and carried a shot of bourbon over to a group of nurses clustered around the radio. 'I have a weakness for the new Nero Wolfe drama,' she said to me. 'Hope those girls want to listen to "The Case of the Missing Mind". See you later.'

Lt Rawlins sat alone at a table in a corner. When he saw me he rose and pulled out a chair, beckoning me to join him.

'Have a seat,' he said. 'In an hour there won't be one available. Can I get you a drink?'

'Yes, thank you,' I said, sitting down.

'Martini?' Lt Rawlins asked me. 'That's your poison, right?'

'Please,' I said.

'Vermouth? Olive?'

'A wisp of vermouth,' I said.

'Coming up.'

Rawlins went to the bar, leaning on it while he waited for my drink. I noticed that he got his own poison topped up while he waited for mine.

Rawlins brought me my martini and set it down in front of me with a flourish before he reseated himself. Turning his glass around and around in his hand he said, 'If you think I'm a drunk you're not mistaken.'

'I've not seen you unable to do your job.'

'It's drinking that lets me live with this job,' he said. 'You see, my father and my brother died at Pearl Harbor. They were serving on the USS *Arizona*. My father was a trumpeter in a unit of the navy band on board. The band had just come out on deck to play while the flag was raised when the Japs attacked. My brother was a seaman first class, only eighteen years old.'

'Oh, I'm so sorry,' I said. I wasn't a crier, but I felt tears well up in my eyes. I might be a drunk too, if something like that had happened to me.

'You deserved some explanation of what you saw this morning,' Rawlins said.

'I don't think you're the only man in uniform who spikes his morning coffee,' I said. 'Besides, it's none of my business.'

'Did you know that twenty-three sets of brothers died on the *Arizona*?' he asked.

'No! How awful.'

'Yes. But the worst of this entire story, my mother petitioned the War Department to keep me stateside since I'm, as they so descriptively put it, the last of my name. I argued with her until I lost my voice, then I cried, but she went ahead and did it anyway.'

'I thought it was a given that a last remaining son was exempt from combat.'

'No,' he said, 'the family has to request it. Hardly anyone does. I started drinking, not because my father and brother died, but when I realized I wasn't going to be permitted to avenge them.'

He tapped the base of his empty shot glass on the table. 'Then my drinking was noticed by my commanding officer, which led to a stateside assignment guarding a bunch of Germans and Italians who will live in relative comfort until they go home someday. And sleep and eat well while they wait. This is what I do instead of killing as many Germans or Japs as I can get in my sights.'

I couldn't judge Rawlins. I'd discovered martinis when I came to Washington after living among Southern Baptist teetotalers my entire life. I'd never had more than two in an evening yet, but who knew what might happen that would tip me over to three? What if Joe had been the person the JDC sent to Lisbon to replace their murdered man?

'Please have another drink if you like,' I said to Rawlins. 'I'm not keeping watch over you.'

'Thanks,' he said, turning the tumbler upside down on the table. 'But I've had my limit. I do have a limit, even if it kicks in after I'm blotto!'

'Does it help?' I said.

'What?'

'The drinking. Does it help you cope?'

'Oh, yes.'

Chantal came through the door and saw us. Rawlins beckoned him over to our table. He joined us after picking up a drink at the bar, smiling widely.

'What is it?' Rawlins asked.

'The FBI has caught Hans Marek,' he said. 'Not far from here.'

'That was quick work,' Rawlins said. 'Where is he now?'

'Agent Williams brought him back to the stockade person-ally, in one those big cars with the FBI emblem on the door.'

'Where did they find him?' I asked.

Chantal had to hide his laughter behind a hand until he could answer.

'At the bus station in Odenton. He was sitting innocently in a section of the waiting room under the notice that read "Colored People Only"!'

Both Rawlins and I joined Chantal in his laughter. I could just see Marek waiting in the station among a crowd of colored people, all of whom were wondering what on earth was wrong with the crazy white man sitting with them.

'This isn't funny,' Rawlins said, as he fought to control himself. 'Prisoner escapes are serious business!'

'Of course they are,' I said. 'But still!' I had to giggle, and shocked myself. I never giggled. Must be the martini, and my vision of a very serious Agent Williams arresting Hans Marek in a bus station planning his next foray into Baltimore's red light district.

The three of us had to wipe the grins off our faces minutes later when Agent Williams came into the officers' club and headed directly to the bar. He ordered a whiskey and soda and spent the next few minutes staring into its depths, ignoring Rawlins' gesture to join us.

'He looks sore,' Rawlins said.

'I think I'll have another martini,' I said.

Chantal started to rise from his seat. 'Let me get it for you,' he said.

'No thanks, I'll get it myself,' I said.

I bellied up to the bar next to Williams.

'Martini, please,' I said to the bartender. 'Easy on the vermouth. Good evening, Agent Williams.'

'Ma'am,' he answered. The bartender set my drink down in front of me and before I could stop him Williams threw down two bits to pay for it. If he thought that would keep me from needling him he had another think coming. After the 'Wonder Woman' jab he'd sent my way I didn't feel quite as reticent as usual.

'Congratulations,' I said, 'I hear the FBI got its man, as always.' I took a sip of my drink. 'It would make a good comic book story, don't you think? "G-men take down vicious Nazi prisoner of war on his way to Baltimore cathouse"! Tell me, Agent Williams, did Captain America arrive just in the nick of time to give you a hand?'

Williams turned to me. 'OK, Mrs Pearlie, I deserved that one. Now we're even. But remember, if Hans Marek can escape from this camp, so could Major Kapp. Or someone as committed a Nazi as he is. That wouldn't be so funny.'

'No, it wouldn't be,' I admitted. 'But you have to admit that Marek's escapes have been entertaining. Do you think he'll try again?'

'I don't know,' Williams answered, taking a slug of his drink. 'But if he does go on the lam again at least we'll know where he's headed! If you'll excuse me now I'm going to join that poker game.'

I took my martini back to the table where Chantal and Rawlins waited.

'So what did you say to him?' Rawlins asked.

'I'm not telling,' I said. 'But he took it well.'

Bahnsen could feel his blood race to his head until he felt the pressure of it at his temples. Sweat broke out over his body, a drop of it collected behind his neck and trickled down his back. He glanced around to make sure he was alone in the tent before he looked again at the card in his hand. It was a German death card, bordered in black, identical to the ones bereaved German families gave out, by the thousands these days, to memorialize loved ones.

It was his death card. His picture, in uniform, framed with a black wreath, looked out at him from the front of the card. Beneath it was an Iron Cross and the words 'Leutnant Alfred Bahnsen, b. 1916, d. 1943'.

On the reverse side, instead of memorializing him with sweet memories and a loving poem, the words were scathing. 'Leutnant Bahnsen was a traitor to his family, his church and the German nation. A miserable informant in an American prisoner-of-war camp, he traded his soul for candy and cigarettes.'

The card didn't pretend to be authentic; it had been made in the craft tent with black paint and a cheap fountain pen and black ink. The image on the front of the card was a skillful tracing of his official Luftwaffe photograph. He had a pamphlet of his graduating class from navigator training with him; someone must have taken it from his footlocker.

Bahnsen thanked God he was alone so his dismay wasn't public. He was afraid, really afraid. The card was a warning, of course. He wasn't an informant, but he was the clear leader of the anti-Nazi element in the camp. Just by challenging Major Kapp, comforting Thomas Hanzi and holding traditional Lutheran prayer services he had demonstrated his hatred of Nazism. He was a convinced Christian, but like every human being he didn't want to die. He was sure heaven was a delightful destination, but he wanted to be on the last possible train out.

So how to placate his enemies? Bury his morals and his religion deep in the dirt of this camp, at least until the end of the war?

ELEVEN

Miss Osborne was snoring. Very delicately, but still snoring. Which is why I had trouble going back to sleep after a bathroom break in the middle of the night. Even though I was exhausted from a full day of interviewing prisoners and a little tipsy from two martinis, I lay in my bed counting sheep. Until the siren at the POW camp blasted into the night. And kept blasting. One by one searchlights flared into the night sky outside our windows. Again!

Miss Osborne was on her feet seconds after I was. We stood on the floor in our pajamas, barefoot, listening to the shattering noise coming from the prisoner-of-war camp.

'Must be another escape attempt,' I said.

Then we heard the shots, three of them, fired close together. I couldn't help but grab Miss Osborne's arm. I'd been fighting in my own way in this war for almost two years, but this was the first time I'd heard gunfire.

Then there were no more shots. The siren stopped blaring and the searchlights disappeared from the sky one by one.

'Get dressed,' Miss Osborne said. 'I can't wait until morning to find out what's happened.'

'Let them inside,' Lt Rawlins said. An MP nodded and opened the gate into the no man's land between the two stockade fences on the west side of the POW camp. Miss Osborne and I hurried inside and found Rawlins standing over a corpse splayed across the broad yellow line that stretched between the two stockade fences. The dead man lay face down in a pool of blood that had already seeped deep into the dirt beneath him. A spotlight from the nearest watchtower lit the immediate area and Rawlins had a powerful flashlight trained on the body. Even with his face down in the dirt I recognized the dead man.

'It's Hans Marek,' Rawlins said, confirming my identification.

A young MP stood next to Rawlins, his rifle in hand. 'He just kept coming,' the MP said. 'Climbing up the wall, dropping over the side, even with the sirens wailing and the searchlights trained on him. I shouted "halt" three times, just like I'm supposed to, but he didn't stop. Why didn't he stop? He forced to me shoot him!'

'You did your job,' Rawlins said. 'Go on back to your post now.'

'Sir?' the young MP said. 'Permission to speak first?'

'Yes?' Rawlins answered.

'The expression on his face as he came over the fence: he looked just terrified,' the MP said. 'Even before I shouted a warning at him.'

After the young soldier saluted and turned away I saw him quickly wipe his eyes with his fingers.

'This makes no sense,' Miss Osborne said, staring down at Marek's body.

'Why would he try to breach the stockade when he's escaped so easily before?' I asked.

'I don't know,' Lt Rawlins said.

I heard a shuffling sound from the camp and turned. Ranged along the interior fence were the German prisoners of war, their hands gripping the wire of the fence, watching us, faces dimly visible in the gloom outside the range of the spotlight trained on Marek's body.

'Get back to your tents!' Rawlins shouted. 'Now.'

One of the men raised his arm and gestured over his shoulder, and the other prisoners obediently abandoned the fence. Rawlins shone his flashlight on the man. It was Major Kapp, of course. He flashed the Nazi salute at us, then disappeared himself into the night.

'Cover the body, and set two guards to watch over it,' Rawlins said. 'It's too late for us to deal with this now. We'll need to let the FBI know what's happened. They'll want to see this for themselves in the morning.'

Miss Osborne and I got little sleep that night. We talked for hours, trying to figure out why on earth Marek had tried to escape over the stockade fence instead of using one of his safer, more creative routes. It was almost as if he was trying to get himself killed. But I just didn't see him doing that. He was a simple, genial man, openly hawking his German odds and ends, escaping so easily twice, heading for Baltimore and a few hours of fun. He was the uneducated son of an ordinary Polish dairy farmer, a supply truck driver who'd hidden under his truck until he was discovered by Allied soldiers when the Germans surrendered in Tunis. Nothing about his death in the no man's land of the stockade made sense to us.

After Miss Osborne fell asleep my mind wandered to the two Germans who 'disappeared' from the Liberty Ship that brought the German prisoners of war to the States. Suicide didn't fit their case either. I didn't have any real evidence, but I thought they'd been murdered, and I was sure Miss Osborne did too. I wondered what Joe had been able to find out about Reichenberg, if anything, and when I would hear from him.

'I hope these scrambled eggs are laced with Benzedrine,' Merle said, 'but I'm not feeling it.'

'They only do that in combat zones, I think,' I said.

'You can get Benzedrine from the PX,' Miss Osborne said, pulling a small cardboard box out of her purse. 'Want one?'

'Please,' Merle said. 'I don't think I can drink enough coffee to wake up.'

'I'll pass,' I said. 'Benzedrine makes my heart pound.'

'That's the idea,' Merle said.

Agent Williams set his tray down on our table and took a seat.

'Are those bennies?' he asked. 'Can I have one? I've been up all night.'

'Sure,' Miss Osborne said, shaking a pill into his hand.

Williams chased the pill with a swig of coffee. The three of us began to gather our belongings to leave the mess.

'Don't go,' Williams said. 'Wait until I finish breakfast, I want to talk to you.'

'We have work to do,' Miss Osborne said.

Williams shook his head. 'Not this morning. We've cordoned off the German section of the camp and confined the German prisoners of war to their tents. We still need to investigate Marek's death. It was too dark last night. Besides, I need your help.'

'Investigate it?' I said. 'Why? He tried to escape.'

'There's more to it than that. You'll understand when I show you the scene.'

'How can we help?' Miss Osborne asked.

'You know these prisoners probably better than anyone else in the camp,' he said. 'You've interviewed some of them already. I'd like you to come examine the scene of Marek's death with me, talk to some of the prisoners. Maybe you'll pick something up I might miss.'

'Mrs Pearlie, I need you to go with Agent Williams, please? You are just as able as I to assist him. And Merle, they'll need you to translate,' Miss Osborne continued. 'Since we can't conduct interviews I must review some documents I received yesterday from our office in Washington so I can get them on the plane back to DC this afternoon. I can deal with those while you two are with Agent Williams.'

I was elated that Miss Osborne trusted me enough to send me with Williams to examine the scene of Marek's death without her. This job was the chance to prove I could do more than type and file, my ticket to a post-war career. I had to prove my worth. Which was one reason I wanted my first assignment to succeed.

As we left the mess tent I noticed the young MP who'd shot Marek alone at a table in a corner, both hands encircling an empty coffee cup, deep circles ringing his eyes. It couldn't be easy to shoot a man you knew, even slightly.

Chantal, the Swiss Red Cross representative, was waiting for us at a narrow gate in the stockade fence that led into the no man's land where Marek had died last night. Williams unlocked the gate and ushered us in before closing it behind us with a clang and locking it again. The yellow line, which was the last visual warning given to a prisoner of war trying to escape, stretched ahead of us between two watchtowers, each manned by two MPs with rifles at the ready.

Marek's body was gone. The FBI photographer had finished his business as soon as the sun was high enough to provide sufficient light and the body had been taken away to the camp morgue.

We stood over the patch of dirt where Marek's blood had leaked into the ground, marring the yellow line's neat progress. None of us said anything until Chantal spoke.

'This doesn't make sense,' Chantal said. 'I don't think Marek would have done this. He thought of more imaginative ways to escape. Why would he risk his life?'

'What do you think, Mrs Pearlie?' Williams asked me. 'You interviewed him.'

'He wasn't a man who wanted to die,' I said. 'He was simple and fun-loving, not suicidal.'

'I agree,' Merle said. 'He was most interested in selling his souvenirs so he could get cash to spend when he broke out of here.'

'He craved a few hours of freedom,' I said. 'But I don't think he would have risked his life for them.'

'He came back without resistance both times,' Williams said. 'Almost cheerfully, in fact. Tell me, did he make your list of possible recruits for your mission?'

Merle and I glanced at each other, wondering if we should answer him. I decided we should. We needed to know what had happened to Marek, for the sake of our operation. I nodded slightly at Merle and then answered Williams.

'Marek was a maybe,' I said. 'After we pointed out to him that if Germany lost the war Poland might be an independent country again, he seemed to consider it.'

'We sure would have spoken to him again,' Merle said. 'Whether or not he would have made the cut, I don't know.'

'I thought that might be the case,' Williams said. 'Come with me. I need to show you something else before we talk to any of the prisoners.'

Williams opened another gate between the no man's land

and the stockade itself. The German POW tents stood directly opposite. The area was empty since all the prisoners had been confined to quarters. Military police, some with war dogs on leashes, stood guard around the tents.

'Look at this,' Williams said, leading us to the stockade fence.

Ranged along it, where Marek must have climbed over and dropped into no man's land, was a row of debris. Rocks, chunks of wood, tent pole stakes, tin cups and dishes, even stools from the tents lined the fence.

'What is this?' Merle asked.

'Think about it,' Williams answered. 'It's dreadful.'

'He was stoned,' I said. 'Driven over the fence.' Marek must have been pulled off his cot, forced out of his tent and bullied over the stockade fence. I had a sudden vision of him climbing desperately to escape the projectiles crashing into his body, ripping his flesh on razor wire, praying that the sentry would be reluctant to shoot him.

'My God,' Merle said.

'That's my conclusion too,' Williams said. 'The camp medical officer told me that the condition of the body was consistent with Marek being hit with rocks and other objects before he died. Stoned is a good word to describe it.'

'But why?' Chantal asked. 'And why didn't he stop running once he got over the fence, where the rocks couldn't reach him?'

'Look,' Williams said, 'there are a few rocks on the other side too. I think the prisoners stood on each other's shoulders so they could keep pelting him. But I'm more interested in who did this. Most of the prisoners had to be a part of it, but the question is who is the ringleader? We have to find him or we'll lose what control of the camp we have.'

And I feared we could never recruit any prisoners for our mission under these circumstances. They would be afraid for their lives. All our work for nothing!

Kapp was seated at the table in his tent with Thomas Hanzi playing cards.

'Good morning. I suppose you've come to question me about the sad death of Hans Marek.' He dealt a few cards to Thomas. 'I'm teaching Private Hanzi to play *Skat*, although I've had to modify your American deck of cards.'

Williams offered me the only other chair in the room, at the table with the two Germans, and I took it. I wanted to be close enough to Hanzi to watch his body language as Kapp spoke.

'We believe that Marek's death was a homicide,' Williams said.

Kapp scoffed. 'How absurd. The man was shot trying to escape. He'd escaped twice before, but of course you know that.'

'We don't think he would have risked his life for a few hours of freedom,' Williams said. 'He was driven over the fence by the rocks and other objects we found near the base of the stockade fence.'

'Ridiculous,' Kapp said. Then he spoke sharply to Hanzi, who picked up a card he had thrown down and exchanged it for another. Hanzi glared at Kapp before he made his move, but I didn't see fear in his eyes; it was more of an angry stoicism. 'We had played a game after dinner, throwing rocks at a target we leaned up against the fence, that's all,' Kapp continued. 'Look, there's the target.' He nodded at a tabletop torn from its legs with a target roughly painted on it that leaned against one of the tent poles.

'You could have built that five minutes ago,' Williams said. 'Besides, the guards would have seen you at your so-called target practice.'

Kapp shrugged. 'You assume that the guards were actually doing their jobs,' he said. 'Instead of playing poker in the mess tent.'

'Let me ask him a question,' I said to Williams.

'Sure, why not?'

I turned to Kapp. 'Why is Thomas Hanzi here with you?' I asked. 'All the prisoners should be confined to quarters.'

'Oh, that,' Kapp said. 'Since I am the senior officer here, I am permitted to have a servant. I have selected Private Hanzi.

Not that there's much for him to do. Taking care of my clothes, shining my shoes and running my little errands takes maybe twenty minutes a day. Which is why I am teaching him to play *Skat*. He's learning surprisingly quickly.' Hanzi could sense what Kapp was saying about him in English from the tone of his voice. His jaw clenched at Kapp's words, but he just picked up the cards he had been dealt and began to sort them.

As we left Kapp's tent Hanzi turned to watch us go, and I was struck again by his looks. The young gypsy was stunning, if you could use that word to describe a man. He reminded me of a young Clark Gable. Except for his bright blue eyes.

The four of us huddled outside Kapp's tent.

'I don't see any point in interviewing the other prisoners,' Williams said. 'Kapp controls them all. And after what happened to Marek they'll all be terrified.'

'If we could protect Lt Bahnsen I think he might tell us what happened,' I said.

'The Lutheran almost-priest? We can't protect him,' Chantal said. 'Kapp would know immediately if we questioned him, and there's nowhere to put him where he'd be safe.'

'We could confine him to the infirmary,' Williams said. 'I'm sure Lt Rawlins could arrange that. We could tell the other prisoners he has the flu.'

'Kapp would never buy that,' Chantal said.

Bringing any attention to Bahnsen would ruin his effectiveness to us as a possible operative. A coded letter from Kapp, protected by the Red Cross, could get to the Reich in a week. Bahnsen knew that too.

'Thanks to the Geneva Convention we don't have options,' Williams said. 'Unless we can prove Kapp murdered Marek, or had him murdered. That's a felony and we could arrest him and transfer him to a federal prison. The Geneva Convention doesn't protect him from that.'

'Who is the next senior officer in the camp, the person who would take Kapp's place?' I asked. 'Steiner?'

'No, it's Hauptmann Beck.'

We hadn't interviewed him yet, and I couldn't remember anything about him from our prisoner summaries.

'Is he SS?' Merle asked.

Williams shook his head. 'No, he commanded a Transport Division. Steiner is the next ranking SS officer, but he's a lieutenant.'

'So if we could get rid of Kapp,' Merle said, 'the next camp commander wouldn't be so hardline.'

'Yes, but we can't get rid of him, unless we can prove he orchestrated Marek's death,' Chantal said. 'Besides, we don't know how effective Beck might be. Steiner might control him.'

'We're done here for now,' Williams said. 'I'm going to tell Lt Rawlins so that he can let the krauts out of their tents.'

'I've got to get to a telephone,' Chantal said, moving toward the stockade gate. 'I need to report Marek's death to my superiors so his family in Germany can be notified.'

Merle and I started to follow him, but Williams stopped us.

'I'd like your help with one more thing,' he said. 'Can you come look at Marek's body with me? I'd like a witness to its condition.'

Merle blanched. 'Hold on,' he said. 'Is that really necessary? Hasn't the medical officer done an examination?'

I wasn't squeamish, having spent much of my life gutting bluefish as long as my forearm. 'I'll go,' I said.

'Fine,' Williams said. 'The morgue is at the back of one of the infirmaries, across the stockade.'

The infirmary was in a modified Quonset hut. The front half held six empty beds and the usual medical equipment. A medic wearing a white armband with a red cross emblazoned on it sat at a desk with his feet up, reading the *Stars and Stripes*. When he saw us he leapt to his feet and saluted, then realized we weren't soldiers and dropped his hand.

'Not too busy today, Corporal?' Williams asked.

'No, sir,' he said, grinning. 'We have one patient, but he's no trouble at all.'

'We need to see him,' Williams said.

The medic gave our IDs a quick glance and then led us to the back of the Quonset hut. Pulling back a curtain that stretched the width of the space he revealed a wheeled portable field morgue. It looked like a big refrigerator, but had three cadaver-sized drawers. A compressor mounted on top hummed softly.

The medic opened the morgue door and pulled out the middle drawer. Marek lay there on his back, naked except for a towel thrown across his privates. His corpse was clean, but his chest clearly showed the two entrance wounds from the bullets that killed him.

'Turn him over, please,' Williams said.

The medic complied. Marek's back was deeply marked, bruised and scored by the projectiles thrown at him by his fellow prisoners as he fled from them. I felt ill, not from viewing Marek's body as much as at the idea of what had been done to him. Yes, he was a Wehrmacht soldier, my sworn enemy, but in captivity he'd been harmless. I couldn't imagine why he'd been tortured like this.

The medic slid Hanzi's body back into the morgue and closed the door.

'What will happen to his remains?' I asked.

'In a couple of days we'll release the body to camp Mortuary Services and he'll be buried in the Fort Meade graveyard,' the medic said.

'There will be a funeral and prisoners can attend if they wish,' Williams said to me.

At least Marek would have a decent burial, I thought. I wondered how long it would take for news of his death to reach his family, and if the Red Cross would tell them how he'd died.

'We need to see Marek's personal effects too,' Williams said.

The medic lifted a locked metal footlocker, painted olive drab and about the size of a suitcase, off a shelf and toted it into the main part of the infirmary, closing the curtain in front of the morgue.

Williams and I unlocked the box with a key the medic gave us and proceeded to sort Marek's meager possessions, spreading them out on one of the infirmary beds. His filthy bloody pajamas, wrapped in brown paper, came out of the box first. The rest of the items had been assigned to him by the quartermaster when Marek first arrived at the camp – clothing, underwear, shoes, socks and a wool coat – and there were a few personal possessions he'd brought across the ocean with him. These included a canvas wallet that contained dingy photographs of what must have been his family and home, and a group shot of his army buddies. I looked at that photograph closely. I didn't recognize anyone else in the picture.

'Look at this,' I said to Williams, holding out the wallet with the photograph exposed. 'Do you recognize anyone? Anyone in the camp?'

Williams examined the photograph intently. 'No one,' he said.

The rest of Marek's effects were items from the PX.

'Four packs of Luckies,' Williams said.

'He told us in his interview he didn't smoke, but he'd pick up his ration anyway and sell them.'

'Probably to the guards,' Williams said. 'The prisoners are rationed more cigarettes than most of them can use.'

Marek also owned a deck of 'V for Victory' cards, a tube of M&Ms, a can of Planters peanuts, razor blades, shaving cream, a razor, a toothbrush and a tube of Colgate toothpaste. Williams picked up a pink-and-black Lava soap box. When he handled it, it rattled, so he opened it and dumped the contents on the white sheet of the bed.

German militaria spilled out. The box held a colorful three-inch-long ribbon bar and a few metal badges and fabric patches.

'This must be all that's left of Marek's merchandise,' I said. 'The stuff he sold for the cash he spent when he escaped. Merle bought a cigarette lighter from him. It had the SS emblem on it. Disgusting.'

I nudged the objects with my finger, then picked up a fabric patch of a skull and crossbones, the SS emblem, which had been torn from black fabric. 'I'll bet this came off Steiner's Panzer black beret,' I said. 'He wears it all the time, but he wouldn't be allowed to with this patch still on it. He must have given it to Marek to sell.'

Williams picked up a wound badge and rubbed his thumb over the raised surface. 'They give these out like candy,' he said. 'Like our Purple Hearts. We can't trace it to an individual.'

'Now this,' I said, picking up an ornate silver-and-bronze badge embossed with a tank and the eagle and swastika of the Reich, 'is a tank battle badge. It could be Major Kapp's.'

'Maybe,' Williams said. 'But there are other prisoners here who were with the Panzer divisions. Like Lieutenant Steiner.'

I picked up the ribbon bar. We had ribbon bars in our military too. We called them chest hardware or fruit salad. They were narrow metal bars upholstered with small square ribbons of different colors and color combinations, some embossed with tiny metal emblems. They represented the wearer's medals and campaigns; he wouldn't want to wear any of these on an everyday uniform.

'Now this,' I said, showing Williams the ribbon bar in the palm of my hand, 'could be traced to an individual. Let me take the ribbon bar with me. I'd like to try to match it with someone in the camp.'

Williams shrugged. 'I don't see why not. How would you manage that? And why do it anyway?'

'We can use the paybooks and the summaries we prepared,' I said. 'Match the lists of decorations and such with the ribbon bar. Marek also had an SS lighter he sold to Merle. What if most of this stuff corresponds with Major Kapp's career? That would show a relationship with Marek.'

'There's Steiner too, he's an SS officer. Or Marek could have picked up some of this stuff from other Germans at a prisoner holding area in North Africa. It could belong to anyone.'

'Look,' I said. 'Do you want to find Marek's killer and or not? You said yourself it would take a powerful leader to force all those prisoners to stone Marek.'

'OK,' Williams said. 'See what you can find out.'

I scooped up the militaria and dumped it back into the soap box. It was all we had to go on that linked Kapp directly with Marek. I couldn't think of another German in the camp who would be able to force the prisoners to stone Hans Marek until he scaled the stockade fence.

I found Lt Rawlins in his office doing paperwork. He stood when I came into the room.

'Mrs Pearlie,' he said, 'what can I help you with?'

He indicated a chair opposite his desk and I sat down. He followed suit.

'I need some reference materials from you, if you have them,' I said. 'We're helping Agent Williams with his investigation of Hans Marek's death. Our team can hardly interview any prisoners of war until the camp settles down again.'

'I'll do whatever I can,' he said. 'I want Marek's murderer out of Fort Meade as much as you do.'

'I remember that the OSS Research and Analysis Branch published a notebook of German ranks and decorations. We distributed hundreds of them. You don't happen to have a copy, do you?'

'We do,' Rawlins said. He pulled out a thick three-ring notebook from a drawer in his desk. 'I haven't used it. It's wasted on us, since the German prisoners are stripped of their German uniforms when they arrive here.'

I leafed through the notebook eagerly, skimming page after page of drawings in color of German medals, medal ribbons, patches, badges and epaulets, and descriptions of rank. It must have taken hundreds of hours to compile.

'Can I get you some coffee?' Rawlins asked.

'I'd love some,' I answered. Then I quickly added, 'Just sugar if you've got it, nothing else, please.' I was referring to the can of evaporated milk next to the coffee pot, but I could tell from the unhappy expression on his face that he thought I was referring to his pint of bourbon.

'That's not what I meant,' I said. 'I meant the canned milk.'

Rawlins went to the file cabinet where his coffee pot sat. 'I'm glad you don't think so badly of me that you imagine I'd spike your coffee without you knowing,' he said. 'Besides, I'm on the wagon until noon these days. Trying to cut back.'

'So no eye-openers?' I said, taking a cup of coffee from him.

'No eye-openers,' he said, taking his seat again. 'It's a beginning.'

'So you're quitting?'

'I don't think I can do that,' he said. 'I'm just relegating my drinking to appropriate times and places. When you saw my pint in my drawer the other day I figured if you spotted it, so could someone who'd feel obliged to report it. I'm not happy with what I'm doing in the war, but I don't want to lose the job I have either.'

'I'm glad to hear it,' I said. And I was. Rawlins seemed like a good man to me and I hated to see him ruin his life.

'Can I take this notebook with me?' I asked.

'Sure. Whatever you need. But why?'

'The two men who died on the crossing, Muntz and Aach. Miss Osborne and I think they might have been murdered.'

'They committed suicide,' Rawlins said. 'That's the official word anyway.'

'Does it make sense to you?'

Rawlins shrugged. 'Does it matter?

'If there was a murderer on board that ship, then he's in this camp. He could be the man who orchestrated Marek's death.'

'That's quite a deductive leap. But if you want the book you can have it. What else can I do for you?'

'The *Abel Stoddard* had five cargo holds. The prisoners were kept in the holds except for their allotted exercise time on deck. Most of them were the Italians, of course, but the Germans were split up into two holds. You don't know their assignments, do you?'

'Holy smoke, you don't ask for much. I can look.'

'I'll help you,' I said.

The two of us went through the three file cabinets in his office. I was reminded of my old job and was glad I didn't do it anymore.

'I'll be damned,' Rawlins said, pulling a file folder out of a drawer. 'Here it is. Hold assignments!'

He handed the file to me and I skimmed the single page inside quickly, just long enough to see that Major Kapp was assigned to the same hold as Bahnsen, Marek, Muntz and Aach.

'Thanks,' I said, sticking the file inside the notebook. 'I'll let you know if we find anything.'

TWELVE

I found Miss Osborne in our quarters propped up in bed with papers spread around her. She was in her stocking feet and I could see that her skirt was unbuttoned at the waist. An empty pint carton of milk with a straw sticking out of it and an apple core sat on the lamp table next to her bed.

Immediately I briefed her about my experiences with Agent Williams inside the camp, our conclusion that Marek had been forced over the stockade fence by a barrage of rocks, our interview with Kapp and our examination of Marek's corpse and his meager belongings.

'Good work, Louise,' she said, cramming her paperwork into the pouch from OSS she'd received earlier in the day. 'Much more interesting than mine, which consisted mostly of scribbling my initials on dozens of papers. Where is Merle? We need his help.'

'I don't know,' I said. 'He didn't want to see Marek's corpse.'

'Is McVey outside? If he is send him out to find Merle,' she said.

I found McVey leaning up against our car, smoking a cigarette. When he saw me he dropped it to the ground and crushed it with his boot. 'Where to?' he asked.

'We're not going anywhere, but we need to find Merle. Do you know where he is?'

'I picked him up at the stockade gate a while back and took him to the officers' mess,' he said.

Lunch! I'd forgotten all about lunch.

'Where did you take him after lunch?'

'No place. He said not to wait for him, he'd walk wherever else he wanted to go. So I went on back to the stockade to wait for you.'

'Find him, will you? I guess check his barracks first.' I pulled a dollar out of my pocket and gave it to him. 'And go to the PX for me,' I said. 'Get me a chocolate bar and a can of nuts, cashews if they've got them. And a soda, a Coke or a 7 Up. As long as it's not root beer.'

When I got back inside Miss Osborne was reading the hold assignments.

'Got your notebook?' she said.

I grabbed my steno pad and a pencil.

'The *Abel Stoddard* had five cargo holds with about twenty-two hundred prisoners spread among them,' she said, 'say four hundred forty per hold. The Germans were split among them in Hold Two and Hold Five.'

'Chantal said today that the prisoners exercised by hold, for two hours a day. And their meals were delivered to them in the holds. So as they came across the Atlantic they didn't come into contact with prisoners who weren't in the same hold,' I said.

'That's interesting,' Miss Osborne said. 'According to this Kapp, the two dead men and Bahnsen were in the same hold.'

'I saw that. What about Thomas Hanzi?'

Miss Osborne shook her head. 'He was in Hold Five with Felix Steiner and Jens Geller. There were others, of course, for instance one of the SS riflemen was in Hold Five too. The second was with Kapp.'

Merle appeared at our door. 'Reporting as ordered,' he said. 'And I bring provisions.' He handed me the nuts, chocolate and Coke McVey had bought me at the PX.

I showed Merle the ribbon bar we'd found in Marek's belongings. 'This was with Marek's things,' I said, speaking through a huge bite of Butterfinger, handing the ribbon bar to Merle. 'I want to decipher it, find out who it belonged to if possible. We've got a reference notebook on the ribbons and our summaries of all the prisoners' paybooks.'

'You think it's Kapp's, don't you?' Merle asked. 'You think this will tie him to Marek and Marek's death?'

'I hope so,' Miss Osborne said. 'It would solve many problems for us. But we need to do the work. I recognize some of these ribbons without looking them up, they're common. The first is solid blue, it's a four-year service ribbon – see the tiny SS badge on it? The owner has four years of service in the Waffen SS.'

'That fits Steiner too,' I said.

'It does. Now the next ribbon on the bar, the one with the wide red stripe and narrow white and black stripes bordering it; this represents the Iron Cross second class. Also common, especially among SS officers.'

I leafed through both Steiner's and Kapp's paybook summaries. 'They both had one,' I said.

'The next one has a thick black stripe bordered with red and white stripes and a tiny emblem of crossed swords,' she said.

'That's a War Merit Cross second class for combatants,' Merle said, finding a picture of the ribbon in the reference notebook.

'They both have one of those too,' I said, referring to the men's paybooks.

'The next one, the narrow black, red and green stripes separated by white ones, that's the German African Campaign Medal,' Miss Osborne said.

'Kapp and Steiner' I said. 'And most of the other officers in the camp.'

'All right. The next ribbon has a wide red stripe bordered by two wide black stripes, and a tiny tank glued to it.'

Merle leafed through the notebook. I found myself holding my breath.

'It's the Sudetenland Commemorative Medal! With a tank combat emblem!' he said.

'Yes!' I said. 'It's Kapp! Not Steiner. According to Steiner's papers he was never in the Sudetenland!'

'Is there anything in Kapp's summary about Reichenberg?' Miss Osborne asked.

I read through the two pages. 'Yes,' I said, 'he was assigned to the Reich Security Main Office in Reichenberg from 1939 to 1941, before he was sent to North Africa.' I quickly checked Muntz and Aach's summaries. 'And Kapp was in Reichenberg before Muntz and Aach were drafted.'

'That doesn't mean Kapp knew them,' Merle said.

'Calm down, both of you,' Miss Osborne said. 'Let's check the last ribbon. It could still exclude Kapp. It's a wide red one bordered with skinny white and black stripes.'

'The Czechoslovakian March, 1938,' Merle said.

'That's not mentioned in his summary,' I said. 'But we know he was in Reichenberg in 1939, so he must have arrived with the German forces in 1938. This ribbon bar belonged to Major Kapp. And Marek also had a tank combat badge; it's back in the box that holds his belongings. I'll bet it belonged to Kapp too.'

'It could be Steiner's – he was in a Panzer division,' Merle said.

'He was in signals,' Miss Osborne said. 'I'm don't think he would be eligible for a combat badge.'

'Don't forget that nasty SS cigarette lighter you bought off Marek, Merle,' I said. 'That could have been Kapp's too. Remember, after Marek's death when we questioned Kapp, Thomas Hanzi lit Kapp's cigarette with a match. And Steiner doesn't smoke.'

Miss Osborne held up her hand. 'Hold it,' she said, 'you're stringing together too many coincidences because you want to charge Major Kapp with Marek's murder. Just because Marek owned these items that once belonged to Major Kapp doesn't mean Kapp killed him.'

'But why would Marek have them in the first place?' Merle asked. 'Kapp doesn't strike me as the kind of person who'd give his war mementos to Marek out of the kindness of his heart.'

'It was a payment! Don't you see!' I said. 'Kapp had no money, it was confiscated from him when he was processed. He paid Marek for something.'

'Louise, really,' Miss Osborne said. 'You don't know that. You want Kapp charged with Marek's murder so you're cobbling together a case against him from fragments. Besides, what was his motive?'

'Once we find out who did the murder, the motive will be obvious,' I said.

'Ah,' she said. 'You're a disciple of Mr Holmes, are you?

Of course there's nothing I would like better than to see Major Kapp in jail and out of this camp. But this is America, and you must have concrete evidence, even against a Nazi SS officer, in order to charge him with murder. Besides, the Swiss Legation will be all over us for violating the Geneva Convention if we charge him without proof.'

'So what do we do?' Merle said.

'Tell Agent Williams and Lt Rawlins what we've learned,' Miss Osborne said. 'Williams is the FBI agent stationed here, it's his responsibility. He has the resources to use the information we've gathered. Now let's pack these papers up and have a drink before dinner. We're going to the German prisoners' mess for dinner tonight.'

Miss Osborne dug around in her valise for her flask of bourbon and I found my martini fixings. I mixed my drink, if mixing was a term that could be used so lightly, while Miss Osborne poured a couple of jiggers of bourbon into her tumbler and a shot glass Merle had palmed from the officers' club.

'Oh, Louise,' Miss Osborne said, 'I almost forgot. You got a letter. When I was at the mailroom getting the OSS pouch they gave it to me.'

She dug into the pouch and retrieved the envelope, which she passed over to me.

It was from Joe. I ripped the envelope open and pulled out two sheets of cheap stationery covered in Joe's elegant handwriting. It shows how focused I was on Marek's death that I skimmed over the sweet bits to find out if Joe had found any answers to my question about Reichenberg. He had, and what I read made me feel ice cold with apprehension. Now, how to tell Miss Osborne? Because I had to inform her that I'd asked my lover, who worked for the covert organization JDC, to find out what he could about Aach and Muntz's address in Reichenberg. If that was a breach of security, and I was sure it was, I just had to pray she didn't fire me.

'Miss Osborne?' I asked. 'I need to tell you something.'

'That sounds ominous. What?' she asked.

'Well, first I need to say—'

'Spit it out,' she said. 'What is it?'

'I asked a Czech refugee friend of mine about Reichenberg, and where our two dead prisoners of war lived. That's all; I didn't tell him anything about our operation or why I might want to know.'

Miss Osborne looked interested, not angry, thank goodness. 'As long as you revealed nothing confidential to him I'll excuse you. I'll take your word that he's trustworthy. What did he say?' she asked.

'He didn't know the city, so he said he could ask some of his friends,' I said, feeling my heart sink, wondering if that was excusable too.

'He must have found something, or you wouldn't be sputtering about like this,' Miss Osborne said. 'What did he learn?'

'The address where the two men lived, one of his friends knew exactly where it was. It was a small block of flats, but the flats had individual addresses.'

'So they shared a place,' Miss Osborne said. 'OK. They were roommates. Interesting.'

'There's more. It was what he called a bohemian neighborhood. On the edge of a red-light district.'

'Could be a worse place to live,' Merle said, muttering into his drink.

'A male red-light district,' I said. I looked down at the letter so I could pronounce the German words correctly. '*Der Bubistrich.*'

'My God,' Merle said. 'The murdered men were pansies!'

'Don't use that expression, please, Merle. The correct term is homosexual. Some people are,' Miss Osborne said. 'Does your friend say anything else?' she said to me.

'Just that the area was known for, well, its colorful subculture,' I said. 'You know, costume balls, jazz clubs, parades, things like that.'

'If it was anything like Berlin before the war,' Miss Osborne said, 'colorful would be a mild word to describe it. I would choose uninhibited, or even hedonistic. And it wasn't just homosexuals reveling in those clubs, either. Celebrities and rich people flocked to Berlin before the Nazis took power. I remember seeing a magazine picture of Marlene Dietrich with Marc Chagall at the Silhouette club.'

'When I was reading news clippings at the Registry, trying to find out more about Reichenberg, I saw an ad for a nightclub that fits that description. I've never seen anything like it in any newspaper in this country.'

Merle was open-mouthed. 'Our SS Major Kapp is *Schwül*,' he said. 'A pervert!'

'Did you learn that word from your grandparents?' I asked him, annoyed by his naiveté. I'd once had the same attitude but it didn't make it any less irritating now. 'I'll bet you dollars to doughnuts that Kapp frequented the cabaret scene in Reichenberg,' I continued.

'The Nazis closed all those clubs down eventually,' Miss Osborne said.

'Eventually. Kapp arrived in Reichenberg early in 1938, remember, but the Munich Agreement giving the Sudetenland to the Reich wasn't signed until late September. Let's say he enjoyed the nightlife until the Nazis shut it down. He met Aach and Muntz. Perhaps he had a relationship with one, or both, of them. Then to cover his tracks he had them conscripted to different units. But then Kapp runs into them in the hold of the *Abel Stoddard* on their way to the States. The two men discover their clubbing pal is an SS officer. Do you know what the SS does if they find out one of their own is a homosexual?'

'His fellow SS soldiers murder him,' Miss Osborne said flatly.

'There were three other SS soldiers on the ship and Kapp was afraid of being killed if word got out,' I said. 'Think of the power Muntz and Aach had over him.' Miss Osborne had started to nod her head before I'd finished my sentence. 'Kapp doesn't act frightened now, just the opposite, which may mean he did murder the men who knew about him. And we still have no real facts, but I know one thing for sure. We've got to rescue Thomas Hanzi.'

The beautiful gypsy whom Kapp had selected as his 'servant'.

'Hanzi is in a dangerous place. Remember, during the fight

in the mess Steiner called him a rent-boy. And don't forget the chicken bones Hanzi found in his bed, I'd bet Steiner was behind that. And now he's attracted Kapp's attentions. Hanzi is not safe from either of them,' Miss Osborne said.

'So you're thinking that Major Kapp engineered poor Hans Marek's death, and the deaths of the two men on board ship too,' Agent Williams said. Like Miss Osborne and me, Williams had refused a pre-dinner sherry. From the frustrated look on his face I figured that if it weren't for J. Edgar Hoover's strict instructions to his agents to eschew alcohol when on duty, he would have loved a drink.

Miss Osborne, Merle and I had briefed Lt Rawlins, Williams and Lucien Chantal on our afternoon's work in Rawlins' office before we went into the stockade to have dinner at the German prisoners' mess.

'You've made some interesting comments on the evidence,' Williams said. 'But they aren't facts. They aren't substantiated. We can't arrest anyone. That lame excuse for an alibi for the stoning, the business about the target, is just barely tenable,' he continued. 'And if what you suspect of Kapp is true, he's killed the two men who could have revealed his sexual interests to the other SS men in the camp. Though if he gave Marek his ribbon bar and other trinkets as a payment for keeping silent, we'll never be able to substantiate that.'

'What about Thomas Hanzi?' I asked. 'Can't you do something to protect him?'

'What?' Rawlins said. 'We could send him to the infirmary for a few days, that's about it. Hanzi will just have to take care of himself. I expect he's used to it. Let's eat, and get this meal over with so we can go to the officers' club and get a real drink, instead of that bloody sherry the quartermaster puts out before dinner.'

The meal was a quiet and orderly affair. The only thing I found disturbing was the way Thomas Hanzi waited on Kapp. Refilling his water glass, lighting his cigarette, clearing his plate away so he could eat his dessert and finally pouring his coffee. I was afraid for the man.

Miss Osborne and I skipped the officers' club in favor of having another libation in our own billet.

'I wonder if we can catch a lift back to DC by plane tomorrow, or if we'll need to go by car,' Miss Osborne said.

I wasn't surprised to hear we were leaving. With Major Kapp, a Waffen SS officer who might be a killer, in charge of this camp we wouldn't be able to recruit anyone for our operation. They would be too frightened of reprisals to volunteer. We were done here. Any recruits for our propaganda mission to the German army in Italy would need to come from other camps.

Miss Osborne noticed my disappointed expression. She patted my shoulder. 'Don't take it so hard,' she said. 'There were circumstances beyond our control here. There's plenty of other work to do back in DC.'

McVey pulled up to the curb and got out of the sedan.

'Do you know if we're taking an airplane?' Merle asked him.

'Not today,' McVey said. 'I'll help you get your luggage back inside the barracks and then I have orders to take you to the stockade.'

'What for?' Miss Osborne said.

'I don't know, ma'am,' he answered. 'I just know my orders. But I can tell you all hell has broken loose.'

We dumped our luggage and cases inside our barracks and were back inside the car in five minutes. The MPs at the gate waved us inside and we stopped outside the stockade gate, where Lt Rawlins, Agent Williams and Lucien Chantal waited for us. When they saw us all three of them dropped their cigarettes and crushed them into the dirt.

'What's happened?' Miss Osborne said.

'I'd rather get your first impressions,' Rawlins said.

I could tell by the look on Merle's face that he would rather not go inside the camp at all.

I walked at Chantal's side as we passed by the prisoners' tents. None of them was in sight; they were all confined to their quarters. MPs stood guard outside the door to each tent.

'Tell me what's happened,' I whispered to Chantal.

'It changes everything,' he answered.

We stopped outside the shower tent.

'Prepare yourselves,' Rawlins said. He led the way inside.

The canvas tent had a long pipe stretched across the ceiling with several shower heads affixed to it. One dripped rhythmically on to the dirt floor. An overturned chair from the mess tent rested in a corner.

One of the prisoners of war hung from the pipe, a noose fashioned from clothesline around his neck, his head lolling over his chest, his neck snapped. His features were so contorted I couldn't recognize him. His face was almost black and the tip of his black swollen tongue protruded from his mouth. The man's hands hung loose at his sides.

Merle rushed out of the tent, gagging. Chantal followed him, white as a sheet.

'Who is it?' I asked.

'Major Kapp,' Rawlins answered. 'Looks like he wasn't as all-powerful as we thought.'

'Suicide?' Miss Osborne asked.

'I think so,' Rawlins said, 'he wasn't restrained. It would have been easy for him to use that chair to rig the noose, place it around his neck and kick the chair out of the way.'

'But why would he do it?' Williams asked.

'I don't care,' Lt Rawlins said. 'This ball is in your court. I'm glad he's dead. Just send me a copy of your report for my files when you're done.'

An MP entered the tent and spoke to Rawlins. 'Sir, the Mortuary Services truck is here.'

'Cut down Major Kapp's corpse and transport it to the medical officer,' Rawlins said.

'I'll need to see the body too,' Williams said.

'You're welcome to it,' Rawlins said. 'Now let's get the hell out of this place.'

Outside the shower tent Miss Osborne and I found Merle leaning against McVey's car. His color was good and he was smoking a cigarette, so he must have recovered from the shock of seeing Kapp's corpse. 'What now?' he asked Miss Osborne.

'Now we go back to our rooms and unpack again,' she said. 'In half an hour let's meet for coffee in the mess and decide which prisoners to interview next.'

It looked like our work here wasn't finished after all.

THIRTEEN

I was stirring a lavish second teaspoon of sugar into my coffee when Agent Williams joined us at our table in the officers' mess. He slid into a chair next to Merle with his own coffee and reached for the cream.

'I have a favor to ask you, Miss Osborne,' he said, after a few sips from his coffee cup. 'I'd like to borrow Mrs Pearlie from you today. I need help investigating Major Kapp's death. I can't requisition another agent, and Mrs Pearlie and I have worked together before.'

The last thing I wanted to do was spend any time with Agent Williams and give him another opportunity to learn more about me. I had a vision of my FBI file getting thicker by the minute. But I doubted I'd have a choice, and I was correct.

'Of course,' Miss Osborne said, 'Merle and I can manage the rest of the day without her. Do you think you'll need more than one day? Kapp committed suicide, after all.'

'One day will probably be enough,' Williams said. 'We'll see.' I didn't like the sound of that either.

I gave Miss Osborne the documents case full of papers but kept my notebook and pen, stuffing them into my pocketbook. Williams drained his coffee.

'Let's go,' he said to me.

Williams opened the door to the same Quonset hut where Marek's body had lain. A different medic sat at the desk, writing in a notebook.

'We need to see Major Kapp's body,' Williams said.

The medic looked up. 'I'm sorry,' he said, 'but no one can view the body until the medical officer has seen it.'

Williams flashed his FBI badge at him.

'Oh,' the medic said. 'OK.'

In the back room the medic pulled the center drawer out of the field morgue. Kapp was still dressed. I focused on that instead of his bloated face.

The medic helped us lay Kapp out on a metal gurney. 'I need to see his personal effects too,' Williams said.

'They just brought over his footlocker,' the medic said, nodding at the olive drab metal suitcase on the floor. 'It's not locked, but no one's touched it.'

After the medic left Williams rolled up his sleeves. 'This is what I like,' he said, 'an untouched body. Before some Dr Frankenstein cuts it into pieces. Look at this. I noticed it in the shower tent.' He raised one of Kapp's hands. 'Check out his wrist.' I caught my breath. A band of light bruising, almost invisible to the naked eye, circled the thin wrist. 'And the other one too,' Williams said.

I raised Kapp's other hand and checked it. It, too, showed light bruising around the wrist.

'His hands were tied,' I said. 'By something fairly soft, so it wouldn't leave much of a mark.'

'A napkin, or a handkerchief, was used to tie Kapp's hands,' Williams said. 'Then he was cut loose after he died.'

'So it wasn't suicide,' I said. I supposed I shouldn't have been surprised. Kapp didn't seem like a man who would kill himself.

'He was murdered,' Williams said. 'We need to call the photographer back to get snaps of Kapp's wrists. These bruises are the only evidence we have so far.'

I scratched 'Who isn't a suspect?' in my notebook while Williams went to ask the medic to call a photographer. Kapp had been a cruel and dangerous man. I hadn't been fazed, didn't even startle, when I realized he'd been murdered. When I looked at his ghastly face, almost black with blood trapped by the noose, I was repelled, but felt no sympathy for the man himself at all. Where I grew up the best defense to a murder charge was always 'He needed killin'.' If anyone needed killing it was Major Kapp. Despite the slim evidence I was almost positive he'd murdered the two prisoners of war on board the *Abel Stoddard*, and I was sure he'd arranged the death of Hans Marek. Who knew who would have been next?

When Williams returned we searched Kapp's body, patting him down and emptying his pockets. We found only a folded, pristine handkerchief, a package of cigarettes and a box of 'V' matches.

Next we went through Kapp's footlocker. Like Marek's, most of its contents were items he would have gotten from the quartermaster or bought at the commissary.

A pair of pajamas, socks, a second shirt, a winter coat (so far unused), a second pack of cigarettes, and so on.

'There's nothing personal here at all,' Williams said. 'No militaria. He kept nothing from his German uniform.'

I told Williams what Miss Osborne, Merle and I had learned from the militaria we'd retrieved from Marek's possessions.

'So,' Williams said, 'you think Kapp gave his ribbon bar and badges to Marek to sell? To keep him quiet about the death of the two men on the ship?'

'I do,' I said, 'and so does Miss Osborne. The ribbon bar from Marek's locker matched Kapp's service details perfectly. Merle bought a trench lighter embossed with the SS death's head from Marek. Kapp smoked, Steiner doesn't. We can place all three men – Aach, Muntz and Kapp – there in 1938 and part of 1939.'

'That doesn't mean they knew each other,' he said.

I dived into the deep end of the pool and explained that I thought there might be a homosexual connection between the three men in Reichenberg. The FBI was notoriously biased against subcultures of any kind, whether they were sexual, cultural or political. I didn't know how this might affect Williams' attitude toward this puzzle.

Williams didn't blink at my suggestion, but wasn't impressed with it either. 'That's not evidence,' he said, his arms crossed, gazing down at Kapp's face. 'That's specula-tion.' At this point we were standing over Kapp's body, as unconcerned as if it were a rug on the floor. 'Just because those two men lived near a male red-light district doesn't mean they were fags. We know Kapp was because of his attentions to Hanzi. But we don't know that he frequented the Reichenberg red-light district. Considering the Nazi attitude toward that kind of pleasure-seeking he would have been smart to stay away.'

While Williams went to instruct the medic to keep Kapp's body on ice after the medical officer's examination, I unthinkingly began to fold Kapp's clothing and repack his footlocker. As my hand brushed against the pocket of his winter coat I felt a tiny rectangular box. When I removed it I saw that it was a matchbox from a nightclub, the Tiger Club. Its emblem was a tiger cub wrapped around a martini glass, the same one I'd seen decorating the nightclub advertisement that so grabbed my attention in the Reichenberg file at the Registry. I had proof here in my hand that Major Kapp had enjoyed the sybaritic pleasures of the Tiger Club. And proof that he cherished the memory of it by concealing the matchbox in the pocket of an unused garment.

When I heard Williams returning I instinctively shoved the matchbox into my skirt pocket. I don't know why exactly, just that I wasn't quite ready to share this discovery with him.

'Let's go outside and talk about suspects,' Williams said.

Williams and I sat on a bench outside the stockade wall and watched the German prisoners at their exercises through the barbed wire. He lit a cigarette, throwing the match on to the gravel. I thought of Kapp's matchbox and fingered it in my pocket, still unwilling to show it to Williams.

'So who do you like for this?' I asked.

'Steiner,' he said. 'No question. The guy is a hardcore Nazi. He hates fags – look at how he treated Hanzi. Kapp humiliated him at dinner the other night. And he would revel in being the senior SS officer in the camp.'

'Do you think he could have done it alone?'

'Sure, if he caught Kapp unawares and tied his hands behind his back. I'm thinking he waited until Kapp went into the shower room and overpowered him there. Wouldn't take long.'

'Maybe Steiner gagged him too; we might not see the marks considering the current state of Kapp's head.'

'Let's check his alibi,' Williams said. 'We'll start with the guards.'

'Sorry,' MP Steesen said. 'Nothing I'd rather see than that pig Steiner locked up. But Lt Rawlins put special guards on the man's tent every night after he had that dust-up with the late Major Kapp.'

'You're sure he couldn't have sneaked out?' I asked.

'Two guards, one with a war dog, in front and back of Steiner's tent. He didn't go nowhere last night.'

'There's no point in asking his tent-mates if he left in the middle of the night, then?' Williams asked.

'No, sir,' Steesen said. 'I'd bet my next leave he didn't.'

'Now what?' I asked Williams.

'I'm thinking,' he said. 'I was so sure it was Steiner. I guess we should talk to Lt Bahnsen next. He hated Kapp. And he was protecting Hanzi.'

I didn't want it to be Bahnsen. I liked him. Even admired him. It was odd to think of an enemy soldier in that way, but I did.

'What about Hanzi himself?' I asked. 'From the expression on his face when we saw him in Kapp's tent I'd say he loathed the man. He must have abhorred Kapp's interest in him, whether he shared his sexual predilections or not. It would just draw attention to him, and he already had plenty because of his gypsy blood.'

'This isn't Hanzi's MO,' Williams said. 'He's survived this long by lying low, not by taking action. He'll stay on the defensive, probably for the rest of his life.'

We found Bahnsen sitting cross-legged on his cot writing in a spiral notebook, chomping on M&Ms he was shaking out of a tube. One of his tent-mates snored on his cot nearby.

'Don't worry about him,' Bahnsen said to us, closing the notebook and nodding toward his sleeping tent-mate. 'He's sleeping off the beer we brought back from the PX last night.'

Williams grabbed two chairs and pulled them up to Bahnsen's cot, holding one out for me to sit in and then pulling the other one around, straddling it backwards with his arms crossed over the back.

'We're here to talk about Major Kapp's death,' Williams said.

'His suicide,' Bahnsen said. 'Yes. That surprised me.'

'He was murdered,' Williams said.

Bahnsen raised an eyebrow. *'Ich glaub', mein Schwein pfeift!'* he said. 'How do you know he didn't kill himself?'

'There were faint bruises around his wrist where he was bound by something soft,' I said. 'And we expect the medical officer to find evidence of a gag when he examines Kapp's corpse.'

'What did you say just then?' Williams asked. 'The German phrase, what does it mean?'

Bahnsen swung his legs and turned to sit on the edge of his cot. He grinned at us.

'Literally, it means, "I think my pig whistles". It's an expression of surprise,' he said.

'You don't seem worried to learn that Kapp was murdered,' I said.

Bahnsen shrugged. 'Why should I be? I didn't kill him. But I'm glad he's dead.'

'Because of your friend Hanzi?' I asked.

'If you mean am I glad Thomas is safe from the major's attentions, yes. I'm happy to be safe too.'

'What do you mean by that?' Williams said.

'You know about the charred chicken bones found in Thomas's bed? Well, there were other threats that weren't reported. Thomas woke up one morning to find a noose hanging over his head. As for me, let me show you.' Bahnsen picked up his notebook and shook a card out of it, handing it to Williams.

'It's called a death card,' Bahnsen said. 'German families print them up and give them out as a remembrance when a soldier dies. They usually show a picture of the soldier and have pretty poetry and such printed on them. This one calls me a traitor.'

'So you were threatened yourself,' Williams said.

'Of course,' Bahnsen said. 'I led the anti-Nazi faction in the camp, everyone knows this. But I didn't murder Kapp.'

'Why should we believe that?' I asked.

'I'm almost a priest, as everyone reminds me so often,' Bahnsen said. 'The fifth commandment says "Thou shalt not kill". I wouldn't kill anyone. It's against God's law and I'm committed to His Word, even if I'm not ordained.'

'You were a Luftwaffe officer,' I said.

'I didn't kill anyone,' he said. 'I was a navigator on a reconnaissance plane.'

'Sorry,' Williams said, 'I need a real alibi.'

'He's not lying,' the doctor said. The infirmary the German prisoners used wasn't far from Bahnsen's tent. The only person we'd found on duty was this elderly doctor in an army captain's uniform with reading glasses stuck in his breast pocket and a stethoscope wrapped around his neck. I guessed he'd been trained during World War I and had volunteered to patch up prisoners of war so younger men could go to the front. 'Bahnsen and that friend of his, the real dark fellow, the gypsy?'

'Thomas Hanzi,' I said.

'That's him,' the doc said. 'Bahnsen said the two of them hadn't had a good night's sleep in days. Bahnsen didn't seem too bad off, but Hanzi looked terrible. Big dark circles under his eyes, and he had a tremor in one hand. So I gave them some goofballs.'

Barbiturates. Bahnsen had told us the truth. He and Thomas had taken goofballs last night and were in no condition to murder anyone. I knew how deeply Phoebe slept after taking a Nembutal. Bahnsen and Hanzi would have slept through the night like dead men.

I met Williams outside the stockade gate. I didn't feel unsafe in the camp – there were so many guards and war dogs around – but I was still relieved whenever I crossed through the checkpoint on to the other side of all that barbed wire fencing.

'I found Merle and took him over to Bahnsen's tent,' Williams said. 'We woke up his roommate, who verified Bahnsen's story. Said Bahnsen and Hanzi had taken pills to sleep, pills they got from the doc at the infirmary. He saw them take them. And he didn't hear anyone leave the tent last night.'

'The doc at the infirmary gave them goofballs,' I said. 'I just talked to him.'

'So it wasn't them,' Williams said. 'I'm out of suspects, except for everyone else in the camp who hated Kapp. We'll just have to wait until we get the result of the autopsy and hope it reveals more evidence. I'm starving. Want to get some chow?'

'Not now,' I said. 'I need to run an errand.' I had a suspect of my own and I wanted to talk to him before I mentioned him to Williams.

I knocked on Lt Rawlins' office door. He called out for me to enter.

'Well,' he said, 'Mrs Pearlie. Come on in. How is the investigation going? I hear Agent Williams stole you from Miss Osborne for the day.'

'He did,' I said, 'but I'm afraid we've gotten nowhere. All the best suspects have alibis.' I sat down in a chair in front of Rawlins' desk and filled him in on what we'd found out about Steiner and Bahnsen. He'd read it all eventually in Williams' report anyway.

'So who's left on your list to interview?' he asked.

I looked down at my hands before gathering the courage to speak out. 'You,' I said.

I saw Rawlins' expression change from relaxed to apprehensive in an instant, as if a cloud had passed over his face. He straightened his desk blotter and lined up his pencils and pens along its edge before he spoke.

'I see,' he said. 'You think I murdered Kapp?'

'I think you might have,' I said. 'And I haven't spoken to Agent Williams about it. Much of what you told me was in confidence.'

'I confirmed your suspicions that I have a drinking problem. And I told you how much I hated being at this post instead of somewhere where I could kill Germans or Japs to avenge my father and brother. And how I resented spending my time making life comfortable for prisoners of war instead. And how I desperately wanted Kapp out of this camp.'

'Yes.'

'That's motive. What about opportunity?'

'That's what I wanted to ask you,' I said. 'Where were you in the middle of last night?'

'In my quarters. Alone. But I didn't kill Kapp. I was incapable of it. You know my pledge to cut back on my drinking? To say I fell off the wagon last night is an understatement. I got blind stinking drunk at the officers' club. Chantal and the bartender practically carried me to my quarters after the club closed. I barely remember them tucking me into bed. Is that a good enough alibi?'

'Yes,' I said. 'And I'm glad.'

'Glad I got drunk?'

'Relieved you're not a murderer.'

Rawlins lowered his head into his hands. 'I'm going to try again,' he said, the sound of his voice muffled. 'To drink less.'

I stood up and brushed my skirt down over my legs, feeling the Tiger Club matchbox in my pocket.

'That's all any of us can do,' I said. 'Keep trying.'

Rawlins walked me the short distance to the door and closed it behind me. I leaned up against the doorknob to let my nerves settle and heard him open a desk drawer. I hoped he was looking for a pencil instead of his pint of bourbon.

I was out of good suspects now too. And the last thing I wanted to do was join Agent Williams for lunch. Instead of going to the mess I hiked over to the mobile canteen the USO had set up next to the camp chapel. There women from the towns surrounding Fort Meade gave out food and drink to soldiers who couldn't make it to the mess for some reason. I got the last sandwich, cheese and pickle, and an apple just before they rolled down the awning for the day.

Back at my lodging I found Miss Osborne on her bed surrounded by piles of paper.

'Louise,' she said, 'good to see you. I hope you're done assisting Agent Williams. I need you to look at these lists of the rest of the prisoners of war. We'll be starting to interview again this afternoon. Can you be there? Eat your lunch first, by all means.'

Famished, I ate half my sandwich before answering her.

'I think Agent Williams and I are done. We got nowhere,' I said. Between bites I filled her in on what we had learned earlier today, beginning with our conclusion that Kapp had been murdered, but I didn't tell her about my conversation with Lt Rawlins. I'd double check his alibi with Lucien Chantal as soon as I could find a private minute with him, but I was sure it would check out. Rawlins wouldn't lie about something that could so easily be confirmed.

Miss Osborne didn't seem surprised that Kapp had been murdered. 'He was too arrogant to kill himself,' she said, 'and had so many enemies. Do you think the FBI will ever find his murderer?'

'I don't know,' I said. I watched Miss Osborne light a cigarette, which reminded me of the Tiger Club matchbox in my pocket. The link between Major Kapp and the red-light district of Reichenberg, it could substantiate Kapp's motive for killing the two men on the *Abel Stoddard*, which in turn would explain why he staged Marek's stoning and might help us discover who killed Kapp himself, I suspected in retaliation for the murders Kapp had committed. This was a conversation that would never even begin unless I showed that box to Agent Williams. Which I now knew I would never do.

I knew who had murdered Major Kapp, but I didn't want him to be arrested. Instead I planned to recruit him for our mission. The man couldn't infiltrate northern Italy and distribute black propaganda behind German lines if he was in a federal prison.

And no, I didn't discuss my intentions with Miss Osborne or anyone else. I assumed she would have no choice but to refuse to give me permission to conceal what I knew about Kapp's murderer, even if he would make an excellent agent. But I'd worked with Miss Osborne long enough now to be confident she would make the same decision I did if she were in my place.

FOURTEEN

Six weeks later

t was cold in the interview tent. I wore my coat and gloves, which made handling all the paperwork I'd brought with me difficult. Lt Bahnsen huddled in the wool coat he'd been issued by the Quartermaster's Office when he first arrived at Fort Meade. It was too small for him and he could only fasten half the buttons. Bahnsen's scar wasn't visible at all. It had faded quite a bit on its own, and OSS makeup artists had taught him how to conceal the thin white line that remained.

After Major Kapp's killing we'd recruited five POWs to infiltrate the German lines in Italy to spread 'black' propaganda. Bahnsen was our star. He'd scored consistently well on our psychological tests and performed brilliantly throughout the training process. He'd made it clear that he'd do anything we asked of him, except kill a fellow German other than in self-defense.

'Good morning,' I said to him.

'And to you,' he answered, blowing on his hands for warmth.

'I've got your paperwork here for you to sign.'

'OK,' he said.

'You'll continue to be a prisoner of war even when you are working as an OSS operative. You'll be lodged in the ship's brig on the way to London and in the submarine that takes you to Malta. Once you arrive there you'll be quartered in an Allied prisoner-of-war camp. When your mission is over, after the submarine picks you up off the coast of northern Italy, you'll be returned to the camp in Malta, or to a new camp in southern Italy.'

'I understand.'

'You won't be released until after the war is over, with all the other German prisoners of war. We will take all possible steps to protect you, just as we do with our other operatives.

You'll be given the opportunity to come to the United States if you don't wish to go home to Germany.'

'Got it.'

'Here's your paperwork. If you'll sign it you'll be good to go. I understand you'll be on a train to Baltimore tomorrow.'

'Maybe I can get a coat that fits before I leave,' he said.

I watched Bahnsen scan the paperwork, then he signed his name and handed the sheaf of papers back to me.

'Where is everyone else?' Bahnsen asked me.

'Miss Osborne is in a meeting with Lucien Chantal and Agent Williams. Merle went out with an MP and Jens Geller to buy cowboy boots.'

Bahnsen grinned. 'Cowboy boots, that's all Geller's talked about. This must be the first time ever that an operative has been bribed with cowboy boots.'

'He had other reasons too,' I said. 'But the boots cinched the deal.' I tapped the paperwork Bahnsen had just signed. 'You made an interesting request too,' I said. 'Immunity from prosecution for any felonies committed since your arrival in the United States and while you work for OSS.'

'Lucien Chantal told me that's a standard request,' he said.

'Maybe so, but none of our other recruits asked for it. What felonies are you thinking of?'

Bahnsen shrugged. 'Who knows what I might have to do?' he said.

'Unless you've already done it.'

Bahnsen stared at me, surprised. 'By God,' he said, 'you know! How did you figure it out?'

'How do I know that you murdered Major Kapp? Most of the prisoners were terrified of him. They didn't care that Kapp had engineered Marek's death, they just didn't want to be next. And besides, there were three other Waffen SS members in the camp. They would have protected him. Even Steiner. Much as he hated Kapp, he was SS too, and whatever happened to Kapp might happen to him.'

Bahnsen crossed his arms and tucked his hands under his armpits for warmth.

'I suppose you'd like to know the whole story,' he said.

'I would. I assume you found out about Kapp and his history with the two men from Reichenberg on the ship after it left Casablanca, but I don't know the details.'

'We were all in the same hold, Hold 2, Kapp, Aach, Muntz, Marek and me. It was clear to all of us that Aach and Muntz recognized Kapp from somewhere. Kapp pretended he didn't know them, but he didn't fool any of us. For some reason they confided in Marek, telling him that they knew Kapp when he was stationed in Reichenberg, where they spent many evenings at the same clubs. Aach and Muntz didn't know Kapp was a German soldier until they ran into him on the street dressed in full Waffen SS regalia. So Kapp had them drafted. Within twenty-four hours they were out of the city and in boot camp. Separate boot camps. And the two of them had the sense to be grateful they were just in the Wehrmacht instead of dead in a back alley. Once on board ship the two men weren't in Europe or in the Wehrmacht anymore, they were bound for the United States, and they weren't afraid of Kapp. They should have been. Kapp murdered them.'

Bahnsen paused to drain the last of his coffee.

'Marek told me much later, here in the States,' he continued, 'that there was a cluster of smokestacks and vents on the deck of the *Abel Stoddard* which created a space hidden from view of the rest of the deck. Kapp lured Aach and Muntz there, one at a time, and simply threw them overboard. Marek, who was looking for a little privacy among the stacks to relieve himself over the side of the ship, saw Kapp commit the second murder. Marek had the good sense to back off, and never to be with Kapp alone again. To buy his silence, Kapp gave Marek every-thing of value he owned.'

'What happened to change that?'

'Marek had a guilty conscience. Once in the States he believed he should tell the authorities about Kapp, but he was too frightened. He confessed to me after one of the prayer services I held. I couldn't absolve him, but he seemed relieved after speaking to me. One of the SS riflemen saw the confes-sion through the mess tent window and told Kapp. He guessed that Marek might have been talking to me about the murders and forced most of the prisoners to stone him over the fence so a sentry would shoot him.'

'Why didn't you tell Lt Rawlins yourself?'

'I'm not a priest, but I try to act like one when I can. Marek's confession was confidential. I promised him I wouldn't speak of it.' Bahnsen grasped his body with his arms. 'It's bloody cold in here. Can't we do something about it?'

'I'll see if I can get some coffee for us; I'm cold too.' I went to the tent door and flagged down an army private. 'Can you bring us two coffees, please?' I asked him.

'Cream and sugar,' Bahnsen called out.

'Blond and sweet,' I said to the private.

Back in my chair I waited for the rest of Bahnsen's story.

'You didn't join in on Marek's murder?' I said.

'Of course not, and several of the other prisoners refused too. Geller and Hanzi were two of them. But it didn't matter. Kapp had all the men he needed.'

The private came in with our coffee, and for a few minutes we were warm.

Once the soldier left I asked Bahnsen to finish his story. He seemed glad, almost relieved, to do so.

'I decided Kapp had to die,' he said, 'not because of the men he'd already killed – there was nothing I could do to help them – but because of a prisoner who was in danger.'

'Thomas Hanzi.'

'Yes. I was very aware that Steiner hated Hanzi because he was a gypsy and possibly a homosexual. And that Kapp was interested in Hanzi. He'd already murdered two men because they knew of his sexual interests. How long would he let Hanzi live? What I didn't expect was that Thomas Hanzi was eager to help me kill the major.'

I'd listened to Lt Bahnsen's narrative with little surprise. But when he said that Hanzi was his accomplice I was startled.

'But Hanzi was so, I don't know . . . not meek exactly . . .' I said. 'Stoic.'

'Thomas had spent his entire life being careful and watchful, and subservient if that was called for, but he was willing to use violence to stay alive if it was necessary. We hatched the plot together. It was easy. He enticed Kapp to the shower room. We bound and gagged him, hoping the FBI would buy into his suicide and not bother with the marks of the restraints. I constructed a hangman's noose from a clothesline. I slipped the noose over Kapp's head and threw the free end over a pipe. Hanzi and I hauled him up and he strangled to death. We unbound him and tossed a chair in a corner to make it look like he'd stood on it, then kicked it away.'

'I figured that's what happened.'

'How did you see through our alibi?'

'The goofballs. My landlady takes Nembutal occasionally to sleep. If she does she's still drowsy in the mornings, and if she's had a sherry too it's difficult to wake her until late. But when Williams and I questioned you in your tent you were all bright-eyed and bushy-tailed, writing in your notebook. It was your tent-mate who was still asleep. So I figured you and Hanzi added the goofballs to your tent-mates' beer and pretended to take the pills yourselves. I'm thinking you threw back a couple of M&Ms, am I right?'

'Yes,' he said. 'It wasn't hard to convince those two that Hanzi and I were out of commission for the night. And when we slipped out of the tent neither of them could hear us, drugged as they were. I guess my next question is why didn't you turn us in?'

'What would be the point? You're more valuable to us as an operative.'

'Does anyone else know?'

'Don't worry, I'm not going to say a word of this to anyone, ever. I'm good at keeping secrets,' I said.

'Thank you.'

'One favor, though,' I said. 'It's a personal question I need answered.'

'If I can,' he said.

'You were in the Luftwaffe. Did you know a pilot named Rein Hermann? Can you tell me if he was serving in North Africa, or if he was captured?'

'Why do you want to know?'

'Can't say.'

'OK, yes, I know of a Colonel Rein Hermann. Last I heard he was assigned to the Eastern Front. His English is very good. He flew for Lufthansa, didn't he, before the war? I heard he had an American wife.' Bahnsen started. 'My God, you're not his wife, are you?'

'No!' I said, 'I swear I'm not. But thank you for answering my question. Please don't mention this to anyone.' If Rein was ever captured, he'd spend his time in a Russian prison camp, not an American one. I didn't know how I was going to reassure Ada without revealing how I got the information, but I'd think of something.

'I won't. It's the least I can do under the circumstances.'

'So, I guess after the war you'll be ordained?' I said.

Bahnsen snorted. 'I don't think I can become a priest after having murdered a man in cold blood.'

'I don't know why not,' I said. 'I recall from Sunday school that before he was proclaimed king, David killed Goliath and a bunch of Philistine warriors in battle, and I don't recall that God held it against him. Maybe you should have a talk with Him before you decide.'